MW00414888

Also by Mae Schick

Lila

A Life of Her Own

Five Women Homesteader Tales

Mae Schick

Copyright © 2015 Mae Schick

All rights reserved.

ISBN-13:978-0-9903527-7-8

Dedicated to

The great grandmothers, grandmothers, mothers, daughters,
and granddaughters

courageous pioneers

especially Aimée and Emma

Every tub must stand on its own [feet]

Contents

Acknowledgments

Heartland, a movie portraying the life of homesteader Elinor Pruitt Stewart, is a fascinating and, at times, horrifying true account of one woman's story in Wyoming. I have been intrigued by the early entrepreneurs of western lands since I was a child. When we were growing in Missoula, Montana, our father took us on Sunday afternoon adventures up into the hills around town. Occasionally we came upon an abandoned shack and explored its treasures - a lone battered boot, pieces of yellowed newspaper, clues left behind from another lifetime. It was ghostly and exciting to walk in the footprints of someone who had once lived there.

A few years ago I came across a photo of a sole woman in front of a tar paper shack. Who was this solitary person? I wanted to know more. I assumed the lone woman was an anomaly - one of a kind. I was surprised when I discovered there were many like her. Thanks to important research by Sarah Carter's *Montana Women Homesteaders*, Linda Peavy and

Ursula Smith's *Pioneer Women: The Lives of Women on the Frontier,* and *Land in her Own Name: Women as Homesteaders in North Dakota* by H. Elaine Lindgren, other writers, and newspaper accounts, I found a gold mine! Actual life accounts aided my imagination: women enduring bouts of loneliness and depression, facing threats and violence, and aching from backbreaking work. As I read their exploits, my tales began to write themselves.

Thanks to Janice Kooiker for providing invaluable assistance as the stories evolved. Among other contributions, she detailed the processes of dyeing and weaving, and explained where and how to grow hot peppers in a cold climate! I am grateful to Dr. Horst Herbert and the Reverend DarEll Weist for their constructive comments, encouragement, and enthusiasm.

The lives of intrepid women homesteaders have been almost entirely overlooked and forgotten in the written history of over four million people who took out claims. I hope my stories are another voice for them. As one of the ninety-three million descendants of homesteaders, my wish is that this seminal population of courageous women will find their rightful place in the futures annuals concerning this important era.

Mirna

A Life of Her Own

…[W]omen were often bothered by unannounced visits from men who were looking for food or work and did not always behave as gentlemen when they found a woman alone on an isolated ranch. [Keeping] a cup of cayenne pepper and a corn-knife within reach as a safeguard against any vicious-minded stragglers…could make things hot and interesting for a tramp (page 63).

Linda Peavy and Ursula Smith, *Pioneer Women: The Lives of Women on the Frontier*

"What is it, Dog?" Mirna whispers. Minutes earlier he started growling, a rumble deep in the back of his throat, and he isn't easing up on it. The sound is as steady as the droning from her windmill, only that isn't menacing—just monotonous. On many days, the windmill's drawl is the most conversation she hears, aside from the constant wind whistling and the animals grumbling for their fodder. Dog and the windmill are her constant companions, and she is satisfied with it that way.

Dog continues his low warning. His uneasiness alarms her. As he continues to protest, his insistence makes her edgy, and her ruddy skin starts prickling and chafing at the back of her neck. Then she hears the horses whinnying in the barn.

She glances quickly at the small shelf near the door to make sure the cup of cayenne pepper is still there and pulls the shotgun down from over the entrance. The horses quiet down after a bit, but they still shuffle around skittishly out there. They can't settle down, but she isn't going out in the dark to see what is disturbing them. It is either a wolf, a mountain lion, or worse—a man. At least the hen house is quiet. That means whatever is out there hasn't gotten into the coop. She has enough wood to keep the stove going through the night. A biting wind whistles through the cracks between the boards where the tarpaper is thin, and she thinks there could be an early fall freeze by morning.

She had eaten her simple supper late in the afternoon, before dusk, and brought in a few more pieces of wood ahead of the cold, so there would be embers left in the stove when dawn broke. She washes up her dishes, and Dog lies next to the stove, waiting for her to finish and go to her loom. He stays nearby in the evenings evening until she goes to bed, and then does the same. During the day, he follows her every move. She is hanging up the damp towel, when he suddenly begins to growl.

She quickly douses the flame in the saucer lamp and positions herself in the complaining rocker, putting the shotgun in her lap and pointing it toward the door. As she sinks down into it, the chair moans like an arthritic rancher whose bones creak from abuse. She pulls the nappy wool blanket over her legs. It is her only handmade possession from Mama. She brought it with her when she got away from the family farm, but the strands of fabric, once colorful red and gold, skillfully woven, are vivid only in her memory.

Dog moves to the braided rug next to her chair. Mirna made the carpet from used flour sacks she dyed brown and wove together. From Mama she learned to use dandelion roots that added a hint of ochre. If she desires a deeper umber, she uses coffee grounds. She soaks her sacks in a mixture of four parts water to one part vinegar then lets them simmer for one hour, after which she rinses them and squeezes out the excess water.

It is a tedious process. After they come out of the first bath, she rinses them again in water until it runs clear. While the sacks are still wet, she puts them back into the mixture and waits while they simmer. When she arrives at a rich shade of brown, a smile swallows up her ample cheeks.

She had not been settled in Montana for more than three months when she discovered that many of the townswomen, otherwise prudent and thrifty, threw their used sacks away. She laughed outright in the middle of the main street of Lewistown and then quickly covered her grin to hide her ebullience. She nearly shouted with joy at finding treasure worth as much as a long-forgotten bank account. After seeing her rummage through trash, the townswomen started saving their sacks and leaving them behind Hendrickson's store for her to retrieve when she came in for supplies.

As her stockpile grew, she began searching for wood pieces to build a simple loom. It took her several months to find enough materials, mostly from abandoned homesteads. These families had tried to survive but used up all their energy and will and depleted their meager savings. They silently disappeared, leaving behind remnants of a once hopeful future. She tried to build the loom on the same design of her mama's; however, she was limited by the amount and type of materials she could find, so she designed a simple table loom.

During the months before she furtively fled Indiana, she plotted and planned, secretly accumulating tools and dry staples. She measured a pot before adding it to her growing but sparse collection. First, and most important, it must fit inside Mama's weaving trunk and not occupy too much space. It couldn't have a long handle or stand too tall, yet it must have a thick bottom, strong walls, and a tight-fitting lid. Second, before it was added to the other contents, she considered how many ways she could use it for other purposes, such as milking, dyeing fabric, boiling a rabbit, and making coffee. She considered whether she could manage with only two knives—one for cutting up meat and slicing bread, a smaller one for paring. She deliberated whether she could get by with one pair of heavy shoes but decided she might be making a grievous mistake, with long harsh winters and muddy springs to contend with. She decided to wear on the train all the clothing that she would take with her. Inconspicuously collecting the necessary equipment, she hid it a piece at a time under the weaving supplies in Mama's trunk, and as her list of necessities shrank, her restlessness became increasingly intense. She started to fear that if she did not leave soon, her brother, Carl, would push her too far, and she would explode. She forced herself to leave her scissors in the chicken coop when she wasn't using them.

Everything she would take had to fit in the one trunk. She was watchful and diligent as she stockpiled and shuddered that she might inadvertently reveal her intentions if something appeared out of place. One day Carl came into the house barking that he could not find one of the big knives and demanding to know where she had put it. She told him she would find it, and when he left the house again, she hastily pulled it from the trunk. "I can't be this careless," she upbraided herself, determined to wait until the very end before she added the knife. Nearly every night she woke up sweating from a recurring dream about Carl chasing after her train as it pulled out of the station. She screamed at the train to hurry up and pull away. When she woke she feared she might really have screamed, but Carl did not mention it.

She packed Mama's cording and wool cards in the dried beans and peas; the drop spindle went inside the pot. Mirna covered it all with Mama's shabby blanket, judiciously avoiding the trunk whenever Carl was in the house, as though it were contagious with a horrible disease.

Her departure happened quickly, just as she had hoped. She waited for a time when Carl would be off his guard. She knew it was a matter of time, a moment when Carl was passed out—unconscious and not able to stop her. When that day came, she ran to her closest neighbor and begged him to take her and her trunk to the station.

The early months on her own land were what she had expected, getting her place set up and putting in her crops. She worked constantly, but it was labor for herself, and the sweat and calluses, sunburns and sticky days seemed small drawbacks. Autumn came abruptly, however, and she had to work harder and faster to stay even with her modest harvest.

In her little homestead that first year, during the winter months when night came too early, and she needed to pass the time until bedtime, Mirna took up the weaving. It had a rhythm that soothed and relaxed her, especially when the wind howled like a crazed wounded animal. On the rare occasions she went to town to stock up on supplies at Hendrickson's General Store in Lewistown, Montana, she collected the sacks the women had saved for her and brought completed carpets she had dyed and woven. She was hesitant about approaching Mr. Hendrickson to ask to display her rugs but reassured herself by remembering that Mama had once done the same.

Dog finally stops growling and closes his eyes, but he doesn't sleep. He is flat on his belly with his front paws extended in front of him, his long, elegant nose pointing, like the end of the shotgun, toward the door, while his reddish tail stretches straight out behind him. Occasionally he opens one eye to see if Mirna is awake. She is watchful while also trying to rest. Stray strands of blond hair, the color and texture of laundry left out too long on a clothesline, tumble from the tight bun at the nape of her neck, which earlier in the day had corralled any potential stragglers. Her mannish hands hold the barrel of the gun in a firm grip. Dog whines occasionally like a cranky child with an earache in those feverish hours of night, reminding them both to stay alert and discouraging them from falling into a compromising sleep.

Dog had come to her on his own three years earlier. He chose her, not the other way around, Mirna assured herself. Their companionship was due to his persistence and because he had come to her aid. She relies on his help and his presence now. He has not failed to be a dependable and friendly ally, unlike the men of her family she'd left behind in Indiana.

She had been on her land less than a year when he showed up. She hadn't proved up yet, although she had a field under cultivation, a mixture of wheat and sorghum and flax, and she had hired a man to help her put in her well. When Dog first appeared, it was a fall day similar to this one today, and she had just finished feeding the livestock and milking her one cow. It was a golden evening, the shadows from her windmill and the two small fruit trees planted in the spring elongated on the swaying tawny wild grasses.

When he appeared, she had no intention of taking on any animal that didn't provide some practical use to her, but he stayed by her door for three days. She waved her hands to shoo him away, trying her best to discourage him. Mr. Hendrickson at the general store in Lewistown had advised her, when she first arrived from the train and was getting her supplies for the homestead ten miles east of town, that she get a dog. "Almost all the single ladies here keep a dog to protect them," he told her, but she mumbled under her breath that she could protect herself; she didn't need a dog for that. She wasn't looking for another mouth to feed.

She stayed away from town unless she needed supplies or more flour sacks. In the beginning, she got an occasional visit from Mrs. Andersson, the wife of one of the ranchers. She brought a molasses pie the first time. Mirna didn't invite her in for coffee or even ask her to sit down for a spell. She wasn't familiar enough with sweet foods to develop a fondness for them. She did take the pie, because she didn't know how to refuse it, but it took her three weeks to finish it off. What she had wanted to say to Mrs. Andersson was that she wasn't interested in a pie, but she couldn't get around to finding the words.

"Shoo," she yelled at the dog on the second day after he had first appeared on her land, ambling out of the deep coulee that divided her property in half. She found him sleeping outside her door. "Get away from here, you mongrel," she said each time she came out or went into the shack and had to step over him. He shuffled away hanging his head, his tail drooping as though he felt bad, not because she yelled at him, but because he regretted upsetting her. When he sauntered off into the wild grasses, he moved more like a coyote than a coyote does. He headed up to the top of the ridge near the shack, where he watched her and waited until she went back inside. When she came back out again, she found him right next to the door once more. He didn't give her any pathetic looks, the kinds that make you feel sorry enough to bend down and pat the poor animal on its head or scratch it behind its ears. He didn't even act hungry, or try to beg for food, although clearly he had not eaten much for some time.

"No doubt," she told him, chasing him away once again, "some homesteaders left you behind when they went broke and went back to wherever they come from. They couldn't afford to feed you. Neither me."

The fourth morning, she came outside to find him herding her chickens back into the coop. She found a hole in the wire fencing where an animal, most likely a coyote, had tried to get in. None of her chickens were missing, and she got a good collection of eggs that day. After supper, she put some leftover potato and a bone from her soup pot with a scrap of meat still hanging from it into a rusted metal bowl and pushed it out the door.

She never got around to calling him anything other than Dog. Her two horses were both Horse. She had a mule, too. He was Mule, the milk cow, Milker. She did call the rooster You Old Crow when she threw feed out for the chickens, and he pushed his way through the clutch of hens to be first to eat.

She hired help when she needed it and tried not to feel too bad because she had to have it. It took more than one pair of hands to dig the well. Even the men who homesteaded had to hire help. She couldn't bust all the sod herself to get crops in, and she needed help with the fencing and harvesting. She made a little money from her carpets; she would have liked to sell some eggs and young hens to the neighbors but couldn't get herself to broach the idea. Folks wondered how she was able to keep her place going. Most everyone had to make money in some other way; they weren't making fortunes off their crops, although the past two years they'd had good harvests.

Mrs. Andersson showed up again one day, not too long after Dog came to stay. She had Mrs. Wilcox with her this time, and they had a question for Mirna. Mrs. Wilcox was the neighbor on the other side of Mrs. Andersson. They had each bought one of Mirna's carpets from Mr. Hendrickson's store, and they wanted to know if she had any more of them to sell. Each wanted one more, and Mrs. Andersson had a sister living over in Choteau County, she said, who couldn't stop complaining about her kids dropping utensils through the cracks of her bare wood floors. "She would be mighty happy to get one of them carpets," Mrs. Andersson said. At first Mirna said nothing at all to the women. She wasn't used to making conversation with people, but more than that, she shuddered almost visibly to think that Mr. Hendrickson had revealed her presence in the area by telling people the carpets were handmade by Mirna Brewster.

If her name got around that easily in these parts, it wouldn't take much for her brother, Carl, in Indiana, to find her if he took a notion to come looking for her. Mrs. Wilcox piped up without waiting for Mirna to answer the first question before asking her a second one. They were standing outside the door of her little shack, and Mirna did not think to invite them in. Mrs. Wilcox had a cousin married to a man who was raising a large flock of sheep over in Wheatland County by the Musselshell River. "Well, they have wool coming out of their ears, and what I would like to know is, if we got you a good supply, could you weave some blankets like them Indian trade blankets?"

Mrs. Andersson watched Mirna fidgeting with the knotty knuckles on her hands and looking down the long distance from her head to her dusty boots, as though the questions were too vexing for her to answer. But she was not going to let that put her off, and she said, "Mirna, would you mind if we set a spell and had a cup of coffee? That would give you a chance to think about this idea and for us to rest our dog-tired legs a bit." She moved forward as she spoke, as though Mirna had already invited them inside. The ladies had walked a few miles to get to her place, and they were determined—and curious about Mirna—and they were not going to leave until they were satisfied.

As they entered, they were immediately drawn to Mirna's surroundings. The house was as regular and common as all their little homes were, and it was up to the women who lived in them to make them as homey as they had inclination, resources, and time. However, Mirna's rough wood loom took up a good portion of the space that other women would have called their parlors. It was not a finely crafted tool; in fact, it was downright homely, not like the one Mirna's mama had, the one that Carl smashed in after Mama died, when he discovered Mirna sitting at it and teaching herself to operate it from memory. Many evenings she had watched Mama, not stirring or moving a muscle for fear of missing a step or sequence of Mama's movements as she bent over the loom, entirely immersed in the work.

After Carl destroyed the loom, he forced himself on Mirna. He pushed her down onto the broken pieces of wood and cord and steel and tore her dress so severely that it could never be worn again, not that she would have wanted to have it near her. He left her to nurse the cuts, the blood, and the splinters afterward. She was nineteen and had known from the time she arrived at courting age that she was not likely to attract herself a suitor, and that was long before Carl had raped her. There were plenty of attractive girls in the area to go around before she ever would be considered as a possible wife.

Carl had stumbled in that day, filthy with coal ash residue covering his bare skin and his clothes. He was sweaty when he attacked Mirna the first time. He had returned from the smithy, where the constant cry of a banging hammer and the relentless heat from the forge agitated an already foul humor. Alcohol increased his steaming rage and produced a toxic mixture of hate and grief, wiping out any sense of decency or loving concern for his sister.

Mirna kept house for Papa and him. Carl earned good money as a blacksmith and gave what seemed a fair share of his earnings to the household. He spent the rest on spirits, she thought, but actually he secretly stashed a fair amount from his pay above a rafter in the chicken coop. Mirna discovered this one day by accident, when a rooster got it into his head to cause an uproar in the hen house. He riled the chickens so that they carried on, squawking and screaming as if they were being chased with an axe for the stew pot. She heard their panicky clattering and agitation and rushed out to see what had set them off. When she opened the door, the hens flew through it like convicts busting out of a prison cell. In the commotion, down from the rafter came a canvas bag, coins and wispy feathers spilling to the earth like leaves falling in a gentle autumn breeze. Mirna carefully collected the silver pieces, most of them dollars, counting each as she wiped them off with her apron and dropped them back into the bag before returning it to its hiding place.

Carl had accumulated more than a thousand dollars. She bit

her hand to quiet herself. "How and when," she wondered, "did he start hiding the money?" Spasms of vile hatred twitched at the back of her throat and collided momentarily with a flicker of unexpected hope. "What is he going to do with this?" she muttered. Since Mama died, Mirna had taken over the family accounts. Carl paid in what she thought was the bulk of his earnings. Papa drank too much to have anything substantial left, so an already thrifty Mirna adapted to the circumstances, just as Mama had done. Mama had been frugal and masterful. She had created quality blankets and carpets from mounds of material that, until she gave substance to them, were only fabric with potential. She sold everything she made. Some of the designs she wove into the threads were so unusual that people from the area began buying them to hang as decorative tapestries. Word soon spread about the woman's handiwork.

Mirna waited by her mama each day, hoping she would let her try her own hand at the loom. Sometimes she got to help thread the heddles at the beginning of a new piece of work, and if Mama wasn't in haste to get a project done, she would let Mirna use the shuttle to weave the weft through the warp when her back was aching, and she needed to take a break. As she became more frail, she taught Mirna how to make the beater bar move smoothly, almost without effort. Mirna started doing more of the basic preparation. She observed every move and memorized each step of the process whether she helped or watched. She studied the design of the loom, too. She curled her fingers and ran them over the horizontal and vertical pieces of wood, fascinated by its mechanical capability, how it shifted and swayed, singing with the threads like a fiddle calling out a plaintive mountain tune. She wanted very much to learn how to weave, and she already had design ideas—without ever having sat at the loom to start a project of her own.

Carl continued to abuse her when he found her alone in the house. She was particularly watchful if he came home drunk, but as this was a regular pattern, she prepared for it. She was careful at all times. She kept busy with the work in the garden and the house, but stayed vigilant throughout the day and into the night, for he searched her out and often startled her, leaving the smithy with a plausible excuse and showing up unexpectedly.

When she turned twenty-one, a fact that was acknowledged by no one but herself, she happened to be in the town store buying a bolt of navy-blue damask and overheard some neighbor ladies talking. They were discussing how another neighbor was selling up to move out west to Montana to settle a homestead on the free land the government was giving out. She heard one of them say that even a woman could get a homestead out there, as long as she was single and twenty-one. They laughed. "Who would want to be a spinster out in the middle of nowhere?"

The other responded, "Oh, I don't know that it would be any worse out there than it is here. It would be awful to be a spinster anywhere, don't you think?" And they both glanced at Mirna, who was standing nearby. That day marked the first time Mirna started slipping some coins each payday from the chicken coop and burying them in metal canisters out by her rows of carrots and corn. She snarled, "Fair payment," each time she took a small handful, and she repeated that phrase quietly with each shovel of dirt she scooped up. She scouted out railroad pamphlets with extensive lists of supplies a homesteader would require, and she read an article about a woman who was already very successful in Montana. She wrote for her advice and nearly cried when the woman answered with suggestions and encouraged her to "jump in with both feet, since you are single. What better chances do you have for a life to call your own?"

While Mama lived, Mirna had someone to talk to, although the conversations were sparse and the topics mostly about fiber, dyeing, and weaving. After Mama died, Mirna had very little need or opportunity to speak at all, as she only had her own company most of the time, and she didn't require the sound of her own voice for comfort or stimulation. Any talking with either Papa or Carl produced for her another chore, a derisive comment, or a problem that needed fixing.

In Mirna's snug homestead kitchen, the utensil shelf holds only two drinking cups. The day Mrs. Andersson and Mrs. Wilcox entered the tiny structure, she had a pot of coffee boiling on the stove as well as a savory stew, and the aroma attracted their attention. Once they were all inside, Mirna stood awkwardly by the door with her hands behind her back, pushing one fist into the other as though kneading bread dough. She had not yet said a word. Familiar with the tight quarters of almost all the homesteads, the two guests found the cups in the tidy little area set aside for eating and helped themselves, because they could see if they waited for Mirna to be the host, they might be standing there the rest of the day, or longer. Mrs. Andersson might have said, "Time is a wasting," but she restrained herself, sensing that such a remark would only slow things down more.

The women digested the details of Mirna's abode. "Bertha," Mrs. Andersson said instead as she eyed the fixture over the loom, "Just look at that lamp." Mrs. Andersson pointed to the light fixture. It was a series of long pieces of barbed-wire fencing that had been twisted and tamed until Mirna got them into a horizontal position, long and wide enough to attach to the roof and hang over her loom. She had fashioned holders from canning jars that rested in birdlike nests in the crumpled barbed wire, and these held broad, squat candles. The light fixture was not only functional, as it allowed her to work for many hours in the darkness of winter when the days were short, it was pleasant to look at. The women admired it. "What a smart idea, using barbed wire, for goodness sake, Millie," Bertha said as she sat herself down in the chair at the homemade table. Mrs. Andersson had installed herself in the rocking chair and was lightly pushing the balls of her feet against the floor to keep it in motion. "Mirna, I am going to bring you my empty flour sacks from now on," Mrs. Andersson declared. "What do you think of that?"

"I...I could do it," Mirna said suddenly. She was still just inside the door of her own house, and she didn't lift her head to meet the gaze of the women. They were sizing up the room and its several unexpected curiosities. They had imagined Mirna in a dismal, stark room with few niceties. What reason would a spinster have to make her place of living anything more than serviceable? They were impressed with its hominess, and even more impressed when they heard the sound of her voice for the first time. It was full and rich, with a high-tenor quality to it. They looked at her, waiting for more.

"The blankets," she said, stretching her right palm out in

front of her as though it would take care of any further explaining that they might need. She didn't hear their response, for the rattle in her brain was considering her carrots. *Uh-huh. They'll make a good dye. And I've got the onions. Yes, and enough red cabbage for purple, and beets, yes, I can make the red.* She smiled, pleased for having the foresight to bring bay leaves for yellow, and tea for tan or light brown in Mama's trunk, and marigold, sunflower, and coneflower seeds. She was still reviewing her cache of plants when she realized her stomach was growling, and she was hungry. Dog was looking up at her expectantly, her visitors had disappeared without her notice, and the sun was nearly setting.

Thus began what at first seemed to Mirna the too-frequent visits of her lady neighbors. If they weren't bringing by more wool or used flour sacks, they were loaded with cakes and pies and sometimes even main dishes. Perplexed, Mirna wondered, "Why do they keep coming?" not understanding the age-old appeal of artisans as magnets for the curious and less gifted. The women were also edgy and lonely, often depressed from spending too many frigid days in the tight rooms they shared with clotheslines zigzagging wet laundry across the ceilings.

The husbands on occasion delivered their womenfolk by horse and cart, for otherwise they, too, became irascible waiting for the eternal ice to melt and the morose heavens to brighten. They stayed until the wives were ready to leave and told Mirna that anytime she needed help with her field work this spring, they would come. "Or do repairs," they added. Often there might be three or four women settled comfortably in the center of her house, chatting away in the middle of the day as though they were members of some women's church society. They might arrive carrying their knitting materials or embroidery in a basket, and Mirna shuffled around them, like an observer in her own house, watching these goings on but not sitting among them and sharing in their baked goods or their conversations. Their visits became regular, although Mirna was not a party to any planning and did not know in advance who would come. They each seemed to arrive of their own accord and on the same days. However it happened, no one asked Mirna if their visits were all right with her, and it did not occur to Mirna that she had a say in whether they came or not.

Among themselves, the women shared the doughnuts or cookies they brought, always asking Mirna to come and join them. In spite of inclement conditions, she often retreated to the barn where she warmed herself against her cow as it belched out snorts of icy air. The longer winter went on, the more unpleasant it was for her to find solace among the livestock, and finally she stopped running outside when they descended upon her tiny structure. She put herself down at the loom and began the steady, repetitive motions of weaving. This seemed to calm the restless hands she could not stop kneading together when the women arrived and continuing long after they left.

None of the women were familiar with the process of weaving and were at once fascinated when she began to work. Their busy voices hushed and the hands stopped when Mirna walked through the circle of crossed ankles and went over to the loom. Although it was a crude device, made from leftover parts and fashioned after what she remembered of Mama's, Mirna was skilled as a pianist when she sat down. With those large dexterous hands and long arms and strong back, her movements were fluid and minimal, making the process look easy. The clicking of knitting needles stopped, and yarn went back into the baskets, for the women could not contain their interest. Before long they were huddled around her, watching and murmuring.

Oh, they were inquisitive. "How do you make that thing go so fast?" one asked. "Where did you learn to do this?" And Mirna, for once, had no trouble at all finding her voice as the shuttle flew back and forth across the warp threads. Her voice sang along with the machine's, and before long the afternoon had passed. The sun, if there was going to be any that day—for if it was going to come at all, it almost always waited until four in the afternoon to arrive—was gone, and it was time for the ladies to return to their own little homes.

That winter Mirna's house was filled with regular neighbor visits as well as social calls from people she had not seen before. It was mostly women who came, but sometimes a man or two would show up. They brought their own stools or chairs, and it often got to be so cramped in the room that Mirna and her loom were nearly squeezed up against the wall.

One of the men, Arnold Steadman, was a skilled carpenter. His mother back in the old country had a loom far more sophisticated than the one Mirna had been able to craft from her scavenging. He understood the mechanics of the machine, and with the winter idleness driving him mad, he set about building a floor model in his barn while the ice storms howled. In a few weeks, Arnold delivered his wife and the new loom to Mirna. The day was brilliant as quartz, the sun splattering into a million pieces, but the air was frigid. That didn't discourage Mirna from running out the door without even a shawl over her shoulders to go around the wagon to get a better view. "Oh my, oh my," she said maybe fifty times. She wrung her hands as they worked to get it through her door, bit down on her fingers until she nearly drew blood when they told her it wouldn't fit, then groaned in agonized relief once they got it inside. They put it in the corner, under her barbed-wire light fixture, and she circled the machine again and again in disbelief and satisfaction, much as Dog, when trapping a field mouse, whirled around his victim.

The men analyzed the loom, puzzling over its anatomy, looking for the similarities in its moving parts to those of their farm implements, satisfied when they recognized familiar pieces included in the construction. "Dang it, Arnold, you sure are one surprising son of a gun," one man chortled. "How in the heck did you put this thing together?" But Arnold ignored their questions, smiling when Mirna settled herself in front of the new machine as if she was sitting down with a long-absent friend.

The men liked to roll their own cigarettes, and they did this standing around over Mirna while she worked and they talked. She did not find the voice to tell them she didn't want them to smoke inside, but the wives shooed them out. They said they weren't going to have their clothes stunk up and smelling like chimneys, so the men ended up outside the door puffing away, bunched up like their cows at the water trough.

Dog greeted all first-time visitors with a studied sniff and stare, taking in their scents and movements before he decided with his built-in censor whether or not he approved them for Mirna. He loved the company and ran to greet those he liked and was familiar with when they came into the yard, especially if one of them remembered to bring him a bone to gnaw on for the afternoon. But he only took gifts from the people he trusted, and he always settled beside Mirna once everyone was inside, so he could maintain his watch over her. If someone got into her space, and she wasn't able to move freely to do her work, Dog gave a friendly little growl, nothing threatening, just a reminder, and waited for that person to back off. He never had to remind them more than once.

With the steady supply of wool coming in, Mirna wove blankets that were sturdy and practical and doused with color. They were very useful in the wagons against the harsh winds that blew constantly, both summer and winter, and she had a growing list of customers who, if they couldn't pay in cash, asked to trade their work for a blanket. One man dug a root cellar for her. Another man built a porch onto her little shack, so she could work outside when the weather was good. Still another one promised to build a separate room on her house that she could use as her weaving room.

She began adding geometric shapes to her patterns, and she started experimenting with other local plants and berries for dyes. Goldenrod and tansy produced pleasant yellows, and yarrow and chamomile worked well for the greens. She played with the prairie grasses to get yellow green. When the neighbors brought the whitest wools, the colors worked their best. After she filled all her orders and had the time, she wove tapestries from designs she saw in her mind and longed to get into the fabric, using materials that were not needed for the blankets she finished. At first the tapestries were mostly geometric patterns, but as her young fruit trees grew and started to blossom, she wanted to capture them in her weaving. First she used some of their blossoms to make red dye, and then she studied the tree to reproduce its image on fabric. She used pieces of barbed wire for hangers and took them to town to display. Once she had designed the trees, she wove a hanging of a spotted swainson's hawk on a fencepost. For the black colors she used rusty nails boiled with vinegar and set with alum. She gave it to Mr. Hendrickson, and he hung it up and sold it within two weeks to a traveler from the East who came through on the train.

Then, in the spring, gentlemen callers appeared. First there was the cowboy whom everyone called Buster, because he broke broncs and once had a reputation of being pretty good at it. When he walked, with each step he took it appeared as though he might fall straight over and land right on his nose, although this never happened. He had heard of Mirna through the Anderssons when he came to help with their livestock, and they liked the idea of playing matchmaker to the curious spinster they unilaterally claimed as their own creation. He showed up at her door one early evening in late spring with a bouquet of wildflowers clutched in one fist, his other hand gently on the rein. She was feeding her chickens when he rode up, tipped his hat, and jumped off his horse. She glanced up at him but didn't make a move or a sound. Dog gave him a good deliberate once-over but didn't growl. Buster came over to where she was standing with feed still in her hand and pushed the flowers toward her. Now she was perplexed, wondering if she should drop the seed to take the flowers, or hold onto the seed and look at the blossoms. She never really did give him a good look. Between the two of them, they couldn't find the crank to start a conversation, and once she had the flowers in her own fist, he got right back up on that horse, tipped his hat once more, and she never saw him again.

The widower, Mr. Henry Clawson, was her second caller. He knew of Mirna because of old Fred Wilcox, who had got caught in a late spring blizzard and proceeded to get himself lost. He was lucky enough to catch the light from Clawson's place and rode up. The horse was whinnying, and Clawson went out to find Wilcox sitting like a solid white statue up there. He got him off his horse, thawed him out, and put him up for the night. Clawson couldn't believe that Wilcox hadn't frozen himself to death and decided it was because of the blanket he had wrapped around him. Wilcox hadn't given much thought to either the blanket or Mirna until he nearly died of exposure. It was the missus Wilcox who insisted he take the blanket when he was riding out to check fence posts or livestock. When he figured out that it was Mirna who had saved his life, he couldn't say enough good about her, and how happy everyone was to have her out here, and she would sure make some man a good wife.

Mr. Clawson wasn't afraid to use words. He had been having a devil of a time since his wife had passed on. He had only himself to talk to. It was getting to a place where he was having very regular, long, and what he thought were pretty dang interesting conversations with his horses. Heck, he was having some pretty good talks with his milkers, too, not to mention his two dogs.

He rode over to Mirna's for the first time after the blizzard cleared out, and the ground was beginning to warm up a bit. The horse's hooves pounded like shovels against the still-firm earth, and she heard him coming from half a mile away. She was making a pot of bean soup with a couple of ham hocks in it. Dog gave a glance when Clawson strode up to the open door, the cooking aroma trickling out into the crisp spring air, sniffed him only once, and walked over to his place on the carpet, where he closed his eyes as though the day was too taxing for a protector to ponder.

Later Clawson told old Wilcox that Mirna wasn't one to take your breath away by looking at her but, he said, "By golly, Fred, she sure is a doggone good listener. I think I told her 'bout all my story up to this point." He laughed. "Guess I'll have to make up some more now." He continued, "You know, Fred, I bet she didn't say but two words the whole time I was there. She had them hands of hers goin' on old Arnold's weaving thing, and I bet she didn't even give me one good stare. I ain't so sure she even knows how I look like. I like that woman!"

She hadn't offered him a bowl of soup. She hadn't thought to do so. Although she was accustomed to people showing up at her place regularly now, she failed to recognize the common gestures extended by the homesteading community. But Mr. Clawson, who was on his own at his widower's homestead, was still baffled about how to fix something that tasted good, as his wife had done for him every meal. The aroma from the soup compelled him to say something. "I sure wouldn't mind tryin' some of what you got goin' on the stove there, if you would be of a mind." He didn't fancy riding back to his house to poke around to find what he could put together to call a supper.

She even warmed up some leftover cornbread for him, and the truth was, between her presence and her food, he really didn't want to go back to his place at all, but daylight began to wind down. He asked if he could come to call on her again. She was back at her loom by the time he said it, and she nodded, the back of her head and thick neck bending slightly, the only acknowledgement he got that day.

"Then I'll be back here next Saturday, if you've a mind." He stretched his hand out, holding the brim of his hat toward her broad back. She didn't respond further, but each Saturday since then he arrived as regularly as the train coming out of Great Falls. Their lopsided conversations made it possible for Mirna to continue working uninterrupted, and she stopped only to serve up a meal she prepared and shared with him out of some tacit agreement that stemmed from their first meeting.

Each time Dog saw him arrive, he immediately walked away from the door, went back to his spot of carpet, and soon was snoring like a bugling elk. Mr. Clawson was not deterred by either Dog's snoring or the loom's whirring. He didn't even think to ask Mirna if she was hearing everything he was saying. Winter was going to set in before too long. It looked as though it would come early, by the way the horses were running around like the wind was trying to chase them down.

He had it in his mind that he would soon make a bride of his Mirna, and when he left that evening, he said to her on his way out the door, "There's somethin' important I been meanin' to ask you. I reckon I will mention it when I come next Saturday." He tipped his hat and slipped out into the dusk. That was six days ago.

The eastern sky is only beginning to lighten when Carl busts through the door. The noise from the shattering wood is as jarring as a fistful of rock crashing through a windowpane. The metal hinges, violently ripped from their post, swing madly for a few seconds, pendulums doing double time. Then, slowing, they droop, broken as limbs on a tree where a bear has scratched its back. "Where's my money, you bitch?" he screams.

During the night, the whimpers from Dog had subsided more or less as the hours wore on, but several minutes ago he began to carry on. First he gave out one high-pitched yip, as if he was having one of his twitchy dog nightmares in which some predator was chasing him in his sleep. Its piercing tone was as jolting to Mirna as if he had jerked on her sleeve to wake her. Then the low growling began.

"I hear you, Dog," Mirna murmurs to him. She has a red spot the size of an apple on her right cheek where her fist supported her head for several hours. She flings the blanket off to the floor, fully awake now, although she only dozed fitfully on and off throughout the night. The embers are glowing; the fire has consumed most of its fuel. It is time to put some more wood into the stove, but she doesn't move from the chair. She puts her feet, still in boots, flat against the carpet to keep it from creaking. During the night, the shotgun shifted on her lap. She has a firm grip on it again, and it is aimed at the door. She glances quickly toward the shelf by the door once more to make sure that the cayenne powder is still there.

Then Dog is suddenly quiet. His breathing becomes raspy and fast. He begins to drool. He is almost frothing, yet he sits right next to Mirna's rocker, his eyes fastened on the door, his nose twitching like a rabbit's. The hush is nearly deafening and seems to go on forever. Moments feel like ages as they drag on. The lull is so painful that Mirna is nearly overcome by an urge to drop the gun from her clutch and cover her ears. By the time it occurs—the split second it takes for Carl to explode into the room—the crash feels oddly like relief.

Following through on the same motion that broke the door down, Carl lunges toward Mirna. Earlier, when he edged up outside her small window, he saw her silhouette in the chair. That was when Dog let out his first yip. There was enough dull-gray morning light for Carl to make out her shape. He could see the last few inches of the gun barrel off the end of her lap. He knows what to expect when he breaks in. He knows she is waiting for him; he cannot surprise her this time. He has to create an awful commotion so that she will not have time to collect herself and use the gun on him. He is used to slamming hard things around, pounding them down, and making them conform to his will and his power. He has subdued her many times before and is confident that even the gun she has ready and waiting for him will not stop him.

Another weapon is waiting for him, however, and it is one that violence, suspense, or surprise will not confound or divert. But Carl does not consider this, and it is only as he makes his first stride toward Mirna that he encounters the full strength of its fury.

His first scream sends chills up her spine, and she nearly calls Dog off him. At the same moment that Dog wraps his teeth around the leg and clamps down on it as if it were a meaty bone from a deer carcass, Mirna reaches for the cup of cayenne pepper and tosses it into Carl's face. It is hard to tell whether the bite or the burning first set up Carl's howling.

"Get him off a me," he yells again and again, but it takes some time to assure Dog that he has done his duty. It is nearly impossible to believe that a dog's jaws clamping down on a leg bone could cause it to splinter.

Fred Clawson is feeling mighty jolly. He says he is just the man to repair the smashed-in door, and it is a good thing it is Saturday, too, and his day to pay a call. Otherwise, she might have had to wait "who in the dickens knows for how long" to get that door put back together. "And dang it, with this Montana weather, you never know if it's gonna snow or be a hundert degrees by noon." He rides back to his ranch and returns with his wagon full of wood pieces that Mirna's door will need to get it back onto its hinges.

"I sure would be of a mind to have some of what is cookin' in there on that stove of yours, Mirna," he says, talking just as easily with nails hanging out of his mouth as if they weren't there at all. Dog sits next to him out on the porch, chewing on a bone—with nice-sized pieces of meat still hanging on it—that Mirna took from the pot and put into his rusty bowl.

Sophie

She Writes from Montana

Disapproving neighbors…and unfriendly townspeople…

Sarah Carter, editor, *Montana Women Homesteaders*

"Get down off that horse," one of the women demands. Sophie spotted her before the others when she rode over the ridge. Even in the distance she stood out, her shoulders as muscular as a bull. The women—she counted three others— were a cluster of wasps around the nest of her shack in the valley below. It is nearly dusk, and they should be on their own places putting out supper for their men. All of them have husbands, except her. No doubt that is the reason they are waiting for her.

It was three o'clock when she'd headed to town. She had decided not to take time to hitch the wagon. She was worried about missing a deadline for her newspaper back in Chicago. She had had trouble for days getting her column written. She put the final period in place just as the sun dipped into the westernmost of the two windows in her little house. She collected her papers from the kitchen table and took a last sip of cold tea. When she got her Appaloosa saddled, she remembered she was out of cornmeal and coffee, so she added the saddlebags and set away at a gallop. At that moment, she giggled. If Felix, who right now was probably poring over some legal document in downtown Chicago, saw her mounted and flying over the prairie like a wild cowboy, even his bland expression would register astonishment behind his wire rims.

To say he had been perturbed, not to mention hurt, when she had announced without so much as a topic sentence that she was going to take up a homestead in Montana, would have understated even Felix's superior facility for tolerance. He had wanted to marry Sophie since the day he had walked into the *Chicago Daily Tribune* office. He saw her across the room holding a pad of paper in one hand, with one pencil poking out the top of her pompadour like a single chopstick-in-waiting, another one lingering in neglect behind her left ear, and a third poised for action between her fingers. She was using the last one as a pointer while she read a story to the editor. The editor's eyes crinkled as he guffawed, and Felix wondered if it was because of what she told him, or the way she was telling it. Felix was pulled toward the easy laughter and the casual way she stood shoulder to shoulder with the editor. Her porcelain skin stood in sharp contrast to her hair. It reminded him of the saturated tones of the morning sun on Lake Michigan, and his pleasure in those moments.

Felix was accustomed to the musty halls of the library. If there were women in that building, and they walked near him, and if he considered looking up to observe them, the lighting would have prevented him from sorting them out as individuals. He had not taken into account, before he visited the *Tribune* office that particular day, the abundant sunlight that filtered into the building.

That day he saw Sophie. All the light in the room seemed to aggregate over this particular woman, and to his thinking, it clearly exaggerated the woman's figure and clothing. Felix was not the sort to consider what women wore. It came as a surprise to him when a woman came into his line of vision— through no fault of his own—and his world took on a magical hue. It was a momentary diversion, however, for he did not ascertain its source. Before he could register that his delight came from the sight of a lovely woman, she had already disappeared from his view.

The sunlight that day must have been transcendent. As soon as he saw Sophie in her tailored, long-sleeved white blouse with lacy front and maroon skirt that cascaded over her hips like a waterfall, he decided he was going to marry her. He surprised and embarrassed himself with his sudden urge to see what her legs and ankles looked like. He stood on his tiptoes and peered across the room to get a glimpse of the buckles on her black pointed boots.

The reporters in the newsroom also eyed her, peering over their copy and enjoying what they saw. Even the hand gestures she used with the editor engaged the rest of her body. Energy flew off her, and instead of dissipating in the air, it lassoed the interest and curiosity of anyone who was near her. At that moment, Felix envied those solemn-faced, haggard men who turned into grinning puppies, and her not aware of her effect.

She turned around as if she knew he would be there, several desks like a string of row houses squatting between them, and flashed a smile that bolted through him. Since his legal mind tended to run to the facts, he had already made a not-surprising assumption—his "truths," as Sophie would later label his practice to define the world through logical arguments. He deduced that Sophie was a recent stenographer hire. This assumption agreed with the fact that his sister Ellie was a student at the Rasmussen Practical Business School in St. Paul, where she was excelling. In six months she could get a position like this.

At the top of the ridge, Sophie has the horse reined in, and she is sucking in her breath. She recognizes the bullish woman aiming her horns at her is Bertha Wilcox. The Appaloosa is impatient. He paws the ground as if he is going to dig up a root to stave off his hunger and snorts his irritation. The umber spots on his rump are livid, and he snorts again, demanding Sophie lead him home to his feed. His complaints mix with the women's shrill voices that run up the hill toward her. "Easy fellow," she mumbles, stroking his neck to calm herself.

At least neither Mirna Clawson nor Mrs. Andersson is among the women. Her latest column, the one she delivered to town today, relates the unusual friendship between those two women. Mrs. Andersson was the first woman Sophie met in

Montana, even before she got her shack put up. Not one to stand on ceremony, Mrs. Andersson showed up one day and said, "Let's not stand on formalities, dear. Let's just decide right now to be friends," and reached out with a warm handshake. Almost everyone in the community was grateful to Mrs. Andersson for one reason or another.

During the interview last week, Mrs. Andersson had done all the talking, and Sophie debated about including some choice phrases offered by Mr. Clawson to flesh out her story. He wasn't able to say enough about his talented wife. For Sophie, the difficulty was finding a way to record Mirna Clawson's side. But since Mirna speaks through her tapestries, Sophie stumbled over various adjectives and images to translate the woman to paper. In the end, Sophie felt she had captured the relationship of the two women, and their disparate personalities and unique qualities.

She, like the Appaloosa, is feeling hunger pains as they return from the trip to town. She has in mind to boil up the cornmeal she bought at Hendrickson's store. She has been thinking about it ever since she left town. She plans to eat it as mush tonight and set the rest out for the night to stiffen so she can fry crisp slices with syrup for breakfast, as Mrs. Andersson taught her. Her mouth waters, having it to look forward to. She appreciates the practical tips from Mrs. Andersson.

From her mother she learned how to make meatloaf and to tell stories. In their Chicago kitchen, they tackled the logistics of getting the vote for women while chopping onions and garlic for the ground meat. More often than not, the results meant many burned meals. But Sophie's father didn't grumble. He loved his females, as he called them, more than any suppers they produced, and he regularly told them so. Often, he joined in their conversations after he arrived home and found everyone in the kitchen and the meat not yet put in the oven.

Sophie decided at age thirteen she was going to become a journalist. It happened, not coincidentally, at the same time she was allowed to drink coffee in the mornings before school. Buried behind the early edition of the newspaper, her mother predictably grumbled about the bias in the reporting. One morning, when she noticed that the stack of underdone bacon and black toast remained untouched, she said to Sophie, "You'd better have some coffee, then." It was bitter, but with cream it tasted rich and gave Sophie the sense of being full.

"Come on, you coward," a shrill voice commands, and Sophie shakes her desire for food off as if it were a nasty horsefly. Pushing the cornmeal supper from her mind, she considers turning the horse around and heading the four miles back into Lewistown, but dreads riding in the dark over the rutted road. She can't get used to the night howls of the coyotes in Montana. Shortly after she arrived, she asked Mr. Clawson, who was helping with chores, about their noises. She didn't want him to know she pulls the blankets over her head at night when they cry like babies. The first time she heard them, she thought someone had left a real child near her homestead.

Mr. Clawson assured her, between his hammer poundings,

that coyotes don't eat nice young ladies. However, he did say, "They sure would cotton to some of those meaty chickens thighs running around your place. I bet they'd take a few of them off your hands." He chuckled. A few days later she spied him out in her yard tightening up the chicken wire around the coop.

If she didn't have to ride past her shack and that restless clutch of women to reach the Clawson homestead, she would go there for the night. The women are blocking the way, and maybe they planned it that way. If she could get over to their place, Mr. Clawson would tell her to stay until tempers died down. She could almost hear him saying, "Oh, those gals, Sophie. Just give it some time. Some of 'em is still young'uns themselves. Old Bertha's got a couple of them riled up. They ain't used to someone like you around here. You think things is black and white and ain't going to change, and before you know it, they do. Ain't that right, Mirna?" Mirna would be weaving some purple thread into a tapestry of a hummingbird, the red cabbage remnants she uses for the dye resting on the table. Mirna wouldn't say anything, and as that is almost always the case, Mr. Clawson would shake his head and answer himself, "Yes, sirree."

"They's just jealous ladies, Sophie. God bless 'em. Bertha Wilcox put a fire under them, 'cause she can't keep that rascal of a husband at home if there's a young or pretty face anywhere in the county. Ain't that so, Mirna? It's not just you she's got a quarrel with, dang it, but you're the closest thing to take it out on. If you wasn't alone over there, she'd think twice about it."

It was through Mrs. Andersson that she came to know the

Clawsons, and she was introduced to some of the other women in the community. She met Bertha one afternoon at Mirna's. Sophie wasn't a knitter, so she did not bring a basket of needlework. Maybe that was why Bertha scowled at her when they were introduced. Bertha never did properly speak to her. Sophie could not see why Bertha would not like her. The other women knew Bertha could turn nasty. They glanced at one another but said nothing. Mrs. Andersson was the one person who befriended her. She seemed to understand that Bertha's unkindness stemmed from a deep but unspoken wound. Because Sophie could see no reason for the lack of civility, she dismissed Bertha's coldness as timidity or shyness. *Some people just take a lot longer to get used to a stranger.* Had Sophie known how Bertha's husband went around the county, she would not have hired him to till her fields. Now she wondered if she must take some of the blame. Mr. Wilcox had helped Mr. Clawson when he built her shack. Then he showed up on his own another day and offered to get her fields ready to plant wheat. She jumped at his generosity and felt grateful that her neighbors wanted her to succeed on her homestead.

Oh, he had turned her soil over, all right, did a half-reasonable job of it, too, but she could not understand why he kept coming in from the field as she was writing her column, to ask for a glass of water, then a cup of coffee, then a slice of bread with butter, even after she had fed him lunch and brought him some cold tea. She wondered if he planned to stay for supper, too.

It was late afternoon when Mr. Wilcox finished what he had set out to do in the field. He hurried back to Sophie's shack, then sneaked up to her window to see what she was doing.

She was at her table tapping her pencil against her head, as if by doing so she could knock the words out of it and onto the paper. Thick strands of hair carelessly fell onto her shoulder, and she brushed some loose ends away from her face.

She had promised her editor to send a column every two weeks. The money from her writing helped pay for the work she hired out on her claim. She wrote to Felix that she had found her own particular gold mine. She got so engaged in her stories that she would forget where she was. She could have been sitting on a rock over on the ridge or even on the back of her horse as long as she had a good pencil and paper in hand.

Already she had written about a family who had survived a blizzard on Christmas Eve while traveling to relatives in the next county; in another article she depicted a damaged stovepipe left behind along with a rusted-out kettle, and a black-and-white and starving terrier with one blue eye (the other was brown) when a homesteader ran out of luck and money and had to leave the dream behind; she had even gone to Helena and witnessed firsthand how women were engaging in the state's politics.

But it's the story of Wilma Waters that's so unsettling. It makes her feel uneasy and uncertain about Bertha and her comrades. Wilma Waters was a single woman homesteader, like her, and like Mirna until she married Mr. Clawson. There was also the lady schoolteacher, Nora McCarthy, who was a widow, and Lizzie Vogel, the German from Russia. But it was Wilma Waters who had been targeted, and Sophie could not unearth the reason. As a woman also on her own, Sophie wondered about her own safety. Felix had warned her about that when she announced she was heading out west to homestead.

As thorough a reporter as Sophie was, due to her interviewing skill, she was able to ferret out missing links. But regarding the hostile removal of Wilma Water's shack from her homestead, Sophie could get no information. Poor Wilma had gone on the train back to Iowa to attend her father's funeral. After a stay of several weeks, she returned, and arrived on her acreage just at nightfall to find she had no place to lay her head. Everything she owned had disappeared.

Sophie traveled from neighbor to neighbor asking what had occurred. Not one person came forward to offer information. No one was unkind to her, however, as she probed. A few even invited her to stay on for supper or to have a cup of coffee. But that had been the end for Wilma Waters. She'd caught the train back to Iowa the next day.

When Mr. Wilcox came up behind her, she was wrapping up the story about Wilma Waters, and she was so engrossed, she didn't hear him approach. It was a warm day, and her door was open. Besides, she was tired from the mental work. Before she realized he was even in the room, he reached around the back of the chair and grabbed her breasts as if he owned them. She jumped up and screamed, "Get away from me," and he backed off, acting shocked and insulted. Not to be discouraged, he lunged at her again, and she grabbed for the letter opener lying near the paperwork on her table.

"Well, goddammit," he growled. "I thought with them blue eyes of yours and that gold hair, you'd wanna be kissed. What kind of girl comes here without a husband, anyway? Like you's trying to torment us fellas. You're just a tease, like the rest of 'em." He backed out the door, and she followed him, gripping the flimsy weapon, and waited until he mounted up and rode off.

Felix had warned her about the dangers for a single woman. He said precisely, "Do you have any idea at all about what you are thinking of doing?" She was nearly eye level with him when she wore her boots. For a lawyer, he was almost too pretty to be taken seriously—until he stood before the jury, and his legal opponents, who made assumptions based on appearances, found that facade of beauty did not hinder his ability to articulate his clients' position. From the moment she first smiled at him across the *Tribune* newsroom, she sensed a piece of her future was falling into place. The man who stared back was going to carry her joyfully into old age, and in between that time they would share an honorable and loving life together.

"Felix, listen. You have to hear this." They were walking in Lincoln Park, along the North Shore. It was a warm, late-summer Sunday afternoon and they had been laughing at some boys chasing each other in and out of the water. She kicked up sand with the toe of her boot as they went along. He cautioned her, "Your shoes are going to wear out too quickly if you keep poking them into the sand," so she stopped, and he was satisfied…until she sat down on the shoreline in her skirt, took the boots off, and started along the sand in her stocking feet.

"Sophie," he cried, "now you are going to ruin your

stockings." She giggled at him as if she were ten years old and teasing her obedient cousin who would not break any rules to try something forbidden with her. She lived at the home her parents owned and earned her own money, but the family was careful and practical with their moderate income. Felix knew Sophie contributed a share to help with the two younger sisters. Daisy was still in high school, and Abby was studying medicine at the Woman's Hospital Medical College of Chicago.

"Come on, Felix," she coaxed. "Why don't you try it? It feels wonderful. Your toes will thank you for it. They will make you glad you did it for them." Her grin made him laugh—the same smile that captivated him that first time he saw her. She knew her warmth pleased men, and Felix adored her because of it. She was not a tease. She was judicious, and she tempered her liveliness around men who she sensed could be drawn in with very little encouragement.

"Felix," she counseled, "forget about the boots and the stockings. You really would feel more relaxed if you took your shoes off."

He leaned on his silver cane and shrugged. He would not admit to the blisters developing on his little toes because his shoes were one size too small. He hoped to be stylish and impress Sophie. He came up off his heels to peer down into her eyes. His straw hat obscured his own eyes, so she could not read what lay behind them.

"Are you listening to me?" she asked, looking at the side of his head. Some pieces of his inky hair were sneaking out from under his hat, and she considered tugging on them just to see how he would react. He looked at the boys splashing in the distance. He had the urge to sweep her up in his arms, which would embarrass them both. Somehow he seemed to know he needed to delay what she was going to tell him, but he was not sure why. Sophie's mind ran about two steps ahead of what came out of her mouth. She was not flippant, but intense, and she did not speak without purpose or intent. If she had hatched a plan, he knew he could not prepare for what she would announce.

"I'm listening," he prompted a little too quickly, and she thought he was dreading hearing her tell one of her newspaper stories. It would be gossip about one of her wealthy society ladies who had purchased some exotic bird or other ridiculous creature that was meant to fill in for the banker husband who couldn't find time for family, because his enormous pile of bank notes stood between him and a real life.

"Do you remember Cal at the newspaper?"

"Cal? Yeah. Why?" He was the short, muddy-haired guy with a thick neck and forearms who wasted everybody's time. He should have been fired, the way he went from one desk to the next as if he were conducting interviews.

"Cal is going to quit the paper and go west for the free land out in Montana."

Felix weighed this information, shifting it like blindfolded Justice from one scale to the other. He didn't care one way or the other what Cal was up to. He was a laggard and apparently also a dreamer. Most likely he was giving up a paying job before he lost it. "Cal?" he repeated. "Isn't he the one you said gets paid for doing nothing?" *Why was she telling him about Cal, for goodness sake?*

"Well, Felix, never mind about that. What I did tell you was that Cal gets paid for talking! The point is, Felix, that land is all going to be gone soon—too soon," she exclaimed. "And I have decided I am going to get my hands on some of it before it's too late."

"You're what?" The charcoal eyebrows flew up to the brim of his hat. "Repeat that, Sophie, because I thought you said you're going to make a claim. That's not what you said, is it?" *Please tell me that's not what you are saying.*

"I *am* going to do this, Felix. I told Cal I want to do this, too. And you should have seen his face. I think I stole all his thunder. I bet he was sorry he said anything. He probably wished he had kept his mouth shut."

"I don't even think a girl can do that, can she? I think you have to be married, Sophie!" Even if she could do it, Felix didn't think it was proper, especially for a city girl. Maybe a woman raised on a farm who knew her way around a cow and a horse. *Besides, what about the two of them?*

But her mind was on the conversation she had had with Cal. He had come by her desk and dangled the announcement from the morning paper in front of her. After she read it, she said, "Cal, look here. You don't have to be a man to get free land. You just have to be twenty-one years old and head of household or single. I am two of those."

"What?" he barked. "Are you crazy? This is not something for girls. Especially"—raising his eyebrows suggestively—

"for you. It's tough country out there. Not for a girl who sashays around in pretty clothes and fancy shoes and takes the trolley to work."

"Why not, Cal?" she asked.

"Imagine you wading through muck in heavy boots, or putting a saddle on a horse. You'd be bawling your eyes out in a week's time. Besides, you have to build a shack and live in it. You'd be boo-hooing for your mama in no time."

"You don't know me very well," she snapped.

"Hey, I got an idea. You want to go with me? Make it a couple? That would make things very interesting. The boys here would be jealous as hell!"

"It only has to be twelve feet by fourteen feet," she said. "The shack."

"Huh? That is still a *house*, Sophie," he mocked. "How do you think you are going to do that, little girl? You going to chop down lumber, or haul rocks, or dig up blocks of sod?"

"If you can do it, Cal, I can do it," she fired back. As a newspaper reporter, although a cub, she was conscientious, she was accurate, and she met all her deadlines. The more responsibility she was given, the more she dived in. She loved the work, especially stories about women doing daring and courageous things. Cal, on the other hand…well, it was a wonder they had kept him on this long. It wasn't that he wasn't capable. He was smart, and he had years of experience, but he spent his time flirting with the girls or going across the street to the bar, where he smoked cigars and played pool. If the editor called him into his office and asked him what he was up to, his response was, "I'm on the lookout for a good story. I think something is about to break, Chief."

Sophie knew she could make a go of it in the West. She had read stories about women who were there and doing it. Even the government was surprised by the success of the women homesteaders. They didn't do any worse than the men who were proving up.

Felix had seen the same article that Cal had waved in front of Sophie. What baffled him when he read it was what kind of man would pull up stakes and leave behind all the benefits of Chicago, or any other civilized place for that matter. He would not consider it—not, that is, until Sophie brought it up—because he didn't need to. He had a good education and a position in a growing law firm. He owned his home, although that was partly due to the fact his parents had nearly paid it off and left it to him when they died. He was supporting his sister until she finished school. Still, who would eagerly leave the conveniences of shops and supplies—and the museums—behind?

"Sophie, Sophie," he cried when she repeated to him that women could own free land.

"I just have to be single, divorced, or widowed, and over twenty-one," she cheered, "and I fit that description."

"Sophie," Felix blurted without allowing for his customary time to deliberate. "We could *change* that part about you being single." He stopped her right there on the sandy shore. The breeze gently whipped at the loose pieces of her hair, fanning them like waves pushing against the shoreline, sifting and reshaping.

"Do you think, Felix?"

But he was distracted, because she had put her hands on her hips. Her muslin skirt had red-and-black embroidered swirls, and the hem was flirting with her ankles in the breeze. However, he had gotten to know the tone of her voice, and the exasperating habit she had of putting her hands on her hips when she was about to cause trouble for him.

"Do you think, Felix?" she repeated, planting a stockinged foot against the sand. "Are you suggesting that I am telling you this to get you to propose to me?" She glared. There were vertical yellow streaks in the middle of her eyes, and they flashed like a wildcat's.

"What about the wild animals out there?" he stammered. "Cougars or bears? Good grief, Sophie, do you know why they have a place called Wolf Point in Montana?"

"Bears?" she teased.

"Well, do you want to be a spinster, then?" he retorted. Oh, it was stupid. She could make words come out of his mouth that he didn't even know he had. He was a good lawyer. He knew how to say just enough, not too much, to get answers to tough questions. He sidled his way into cross-examinations with a gentle demeanor, as though the outcome, and his future as a practicing Chicago attorney, were not at stake. But when he got into a discussion with Sophie, he became addled. He bumbled; he was blunt. If he performed before a judge the way he did with Sophie, he would be reprimanded and told to do his homework before showing up in court.

He wanted to interrogate her with about fifteen questions. Who would build her shack was first. How was she going to prove the land? She would have to have help from a man. Wasn't that right? What did she know about building? Or digging or planting or raising livestock? Was she thinking she would find herself a husband out there? Was that the real reason she was going out West? He'd heard there were about seven men to each woman.

He took an official tone. "Have you talked to your parents about this? What do they say?" Sophie's mother probably thought it a brilliant idea, and that if she could, she would do it herself. But her father was a reasonable man. Maybe he was too sentimental with his daughters. He let them decide their futures. Sophie's sister Abby was studying to become a doctor, and Daisy, the youngest, already planned to go to the Art Institute. Well, that was all right. She would dabble in paints until she fell in love. She was the only one of the sisters to mention children in her future.

Was the family so well situated that they could afford for Sophie to give up her income and go off to some desolate hovel and make no money at all? She was going to get a lot of sunburn and blistering and ruin her complexion. Then she definitely would end up an old maid. She wasn't made of muscle. She would have to plow, and her hands would be calloused and rough. In the winter they would crack and turn raw because she'd have to go out and break ice off the water. Where was the water going to come from? Was she going to dig her own well? Who would shovel the feed for the livestock? Did she think they would feed themselves when the wind whipped the snow across the ground, and she had to tie a rope from the house to the barn just to find her way out there and back again? He had read stories about that—people in the Dakotas losing their way just going out the door to feed the animals in a raging storm. And who would be putting wood in the stove while she was outside working? Who would cut the wood for her? Would she be making meals for herself and even have the energy to eat them after she was finished with all the hard work outdoors? And, who, by the way, was going to build the barn for her? Had she thought of any of these things, or was she romanticizing adventure, or worse, fantasizing about a colorful husband? That was a torment, thinking that Sophie would be helpless, and some sturdy fellow would rescue her from her misery.

Well, maybe it will be intolerable, and she won't find anyone she likes better than me, and she will give it all up, hop back on the train, and come home to Chicago where she belongs. By the time she gave it all up and came back to him, she would see him as more than a pleasant pastime and important enough to marry.

"Dang it, Felix. My parents are glad for me! They're not worried about me becoming a spinster," she huffed.

Dang it, herself. Does she know me so well? He had asked her to marry him several times, but each time she responded, "Dear Felix, if I ever get married, it is going to be to you." *What did that mean?* "Let's not hurry when we have the entire rest of our lives. There is plenty of time."

"Time for what?" he asked.

"I want to be a really good writer. If you had to make a choice between working or getting married, you'd feel the same. I want to go on an adventure and write serious stories. Who is it that decides a woman should not work after she gets married? Why are we called spinsters if we don't take care of a husband and children? Who dictates that? You're a man, Felix. Since when can't you take care of yourself? I'm not going to make it my life's work to take care of you. I want to make my own life!"

Bertha's voice booms up the ridge at her. The words ricochet around her like stones. "Come on down here, you little slut!" Her hands are on her broad hips, and her elbows flare out like sails on a ship. "Come on, you little weasel, and get what's comin' to you." The other women are bunched in a half circle around her. They shift like agitated steers anxious to break out of a corral. She has met all the women at one time or another at Mirna's.

Maybe she should have spoken directly to Bertha after Mr. Wilcox grabbed her. In retrospect, she wonders if she should have discussed it straight out. Told her what happened between them. If it had happened to her in Chicago, she would have gone to someone for advice. She doesn't run from confrontations and, like her mother, believes in being fair but standing firm in conflict. In Chicago, she was once teamed with a reporter to cover a story about unsafe working conditions in a meat-packing plant. The man she was to work with offended her at the outset by saying a female shouldn't be involved in grisly topics. Rather than respond to his stupidity, she went to the plant three times on her own, wrote her own version, and handed it over to the editor. He liked it enough to run it on the front page and didn't ask her to team with anyone again.

She is wary out here. She doesn't want to make mistakes in her relationships, because her neighbors are all she has to depend on for help. She is concerned that Wilcox made up a story to cover for himself, and Bertha bought it. She didn't mention the incident to anyone. She could have discussed it with Mrs. Andersson. But she had made up her mind, when she left Felix and her family at the train station in Chicago, that she would face whatever happened on her own. If she couldn't do that, she would admit defeat and give it all up.

In her letters to Felix, she doesn't pretend that circumstances are idyllic. She writes of both the difficulties and the rewards, and she is careful to balance them. She fears if she told him how discouraged or tired she often feels, or talks of intruders like Wilcox or hostile neighbors who have an unexplained system of justice, Felix would get the next train out and attempt to rescue her. As it is, he and her mother are coming for a visit next week. She has been fretting that they will only see things as they are on the surface, like how pitiful her shack appears, and try to get her to leave her experiment behind. The women at her shack down there are getting louder by the moment, and her hands are shaking; her knees, too. Who knows what shape she will be in by the time her mama and Felix get here.

Maybe she should not have taken tea out to Mr. Wilcox. Was that the root of the problem? She had pinned up the hem of her skirt to keep it from dragging on the damp ground, and when she approached him, he stared impertinently at her calves and ankles. She had hurried back to the shack and let the hem down. Within a half hour he was at her door asking for a piece of bread; said the tea had given him such an appetite. He stood in front of her and slowly licked all the butter off it, then devoured it in three bites. Then he sucked on each of the fingers. She tried not to watch him and stared at the floor, waiting for him to go back to the field. She knew men enjoyed being around her. There were men in Chicago and out here who had hinted they would like more, but no one was as blatant as Mr. Wilcox. Until he had grabbed at her, she had trusted men to behave as gentlemen. It was an unfamiliar and unpleasant revelation to need to be on her guard around them from now on.

Felix had asked, "Have you thought about how someone could take advantage of you, Sophie? How do you think you would protect yourself? You won't be able to call out to anyone for help." They were at the front door of her parents' home, and he wanted to leave her with that question. It wasn't that he wanted to discourage her desire for adventure. He supported that; but did it have to be this adventure? Couldn't she take a trip to Europe, visit museums, keep herself out of danger?

But of course she had an answer. "Pip."

"Pip?"

Where is he now? The dog had remained behind at the shack when she went into town. He should be down there, and eagerly waiting for her return. He did not warn her, she realizes, when she came over the ridge. *Oh, Pip. Please, oh please don't let them have hurt you.* Her shotgun is down there, too. Loaded and hanging over the door. *Oh, I would just hate it if Felix was right about me getting in over my head.*

When she told Felix that Papa had been giving her shooting lessons, he was not at all impressed. She'd bragged, "You should see me, Felix. I am becoming a dead eye. That's what Papa says." And she'd laughed. Now, much as she wishes Felix had exaggerated the dangers, she fears she may have to concede his point.

"Are you coming in for supper with us?" she had asked Felix then. He usually ate with them on Sunday evenings, since he had no family waiting for him. Before he met Sophie, he spent his weekends browsing the stacks in the library, or visiting museums. He was in no mood to face her parents, to discuss Sophie's ridiculous decision, and he couldn't bear her mother gloating about Sophie's inventiveness. He did not want to say something to put the house in an uproar. Besides, he had lost his appetite. Roast beef on his agitated stomach would make for a long night, and work would be a torment the following day.

"Felix, won't you be happy for me?" she had pleaded. "I want to do this more than anything I have ever wanted. Aren't you curious and excited about the possibilities?"

He spoke seriously, for it seemed that her parents were not going to hand out any common sense. "All I can see is a lot of obstacles, unending work, and no civilized cultural advantages. Pip may be the only friend you have out there, Sophie." *Unless you make friends with a wolf or some other wild animal.*

The last remnant of daylight is slipping beyond the shack. This appears to be Bertha's cue to act, for she steps beyond the pack of riled-up women. The Appaloosa, in foul temper, tosses his head and glares at Sophie. She thinks she spotted

Pip lying on his side near her well. *Please, oh please don't let him be dead.*

Bertha pauses, and behind her head an erratic halo of fists punctures the evening sky. She takes a few more steps. Each time she moves, the women shift with her. Standing at the bottom of the ridge, she stares up at Sophie. Then, in a sudden spurt, she takes several quick steps. But the ridge is steep, and because of her girth, she must stop to catch her breath. She is near enough that Sophie can hear her huffing. If she doesn't run out of breath in her next assault, she will be at the top of the ridge. The other women swarm as they catch up with her.

Sophie still has enough time to turn the horse around and gallop back to town. It is not too late. She can easily outrun them if she goes now. She has decided it would be too risky to try to gallop through the group to get to the Clawson place.

As they come closer, she feels calmer. It surprises her. Surely they are going to hurt her. *I'm scared, but I'm not going to let them bully me. They're not going to kick me off my land. Not without my putting up a fight!* She doesn't make a move. The horse fidgets under her, and she tightens her back muscles. Up to this moment she has viewed herself as a peacemaker. She wants people to get along with each other. She tries to see the good in everyone. She even understands about Bertha and feels sorry that her life is so intolerable because of the oaf to whom she is married.

So when she suddenly experiences a rush of unexpected exhilaration, she is stunned. There is a force within her, entirely strange and nearly frightful, that has silenced her common sense. If she had the time to consider it, she would wonder how it has come to her, and why it has not before revealed itself. She has the urge to sing in a bold and forceful way like the lead soprano who performed that final evening in Chicago. Felix had taken her to the opera in a last attempt to convince her to give up her notion of going out west. Sophie had been transfixed by the woman's courage in performing the new opera before a crowd of critics who waited for her to stumble or forget her lines.

"Sophie, I know I shouldn't say it," Felix apologized. "I'm sorry. I just have to ask you one more time…"

"Shhh, Felix," she pursed her lips, enchanted with Frederick Gleason's premier production of *Otho Visconti*. She did not want to miss any of the historic 1907 inaugural event. "She's beginning the aria," she whispered, giving him the look she used for Pip when he hasn't had his day's walk. The border collie communicated his dissatisfaction by twirling to the left twelve times, yelping nonstop, and then spinning to the right another twelve times to keep his universe in balance.

She was absorbed in the costumes and sets, studying and memorizing the colors and shapes of clothing. She was fascinated with the tiaras and mantillas. The women wore magnificent tortoise shell combs and feathery hats with festive ribbons.

Their elbows touched on the shared armrest. He smelled her lavender soap and body powder. Aside from her appearance, he loved her curiosity, and the feisty humor that continually surprised him. He wished he could capture her scent and gestures, so after she was gone, he could fill the hole she would leave behind. She sneaked a peek at him, imploring, "Please, Felix, don't ask again. We've been through this how many times?" Her eyes were as generous as her smile. His shoulders sank back into the hardwood seat, and her warmth made him happy for the moment.

Earlier, when he helped her up some steps and brushed against the glossy fabric of her turquoise satin sleeve, he'd babbled about how she looked like a peacock. He meant she looked exotic or something. When he first saw her that evening, he forgot to breathe. He sucked in air as if he had been under water for too long. He didn't say anything in front of her parents, although he was sure his eyes betrayed him when she came down the narrow stairway into the parlor, and he helped her into her mauve opera cape.

He shifted in his seat, while his feet danced a two-step underneath the chair. He had to stop himself from gnawing on the tip of his thumb between Gleason's scenes. He returned to the present only when her hand in the gray elbow-length glove briefly covered his. He had wrestled for weeks with her decision, and he knew her touch was meant to console him. She tugged at his resistance, pleading for his forgiveness, asking for his approval, and above all, for his trust that what was between them would not be lost or broken.

He had helped her get ready to go. He had been supportive. He had maintained the same kind of optimism he held for clients whose prospects were dismal. How many times had he asked her to be his wife? He had stopped counting. He told her he wanted to go to her father. She said, "Not yet, Felix. We must wait."

Her parents liked him. They would be in favor of the union, at least her father would be; her mother maybe less so. Sometimes she seemed as harebrained as Sophie. There had been times she embarrassed Felix with her own girlish notions.

He held out hope that the opera might convince Sophie to change her mind. How could she resist cultural opportunities like this? In the spectacle of the performance she would recognize the many things she loved. The things of which she would be deprived. She would understand how isolated she was going to be. Thus, the opera was a last attempt to encourage her to reconsider. Her trunks and boxes, all neatly organized in her parents' parlor, were ready to go to the Burlington Railway depot in the morning.

Bertha has caught her breath. She is within three horse lengths of Sophie when a sudden breeze flips up the corners of her white apron. The air is cool and smells of rain. The other women, some of them carrying horse whips, scurry in behind her. Sophie's horse whinnies and prances in place.

"Steady boy," Sophie counsels. He snaps his head back and snorts at her then paws at the ground again.

Bertha stays planted for the moment. She commands Sophie, "Get off that horse, I said." The women repeat the command.

"Bertha," Sophie asks, "what is this about?"

"Don't play dumb with me, Missy," and her voice rises.

"I'm not dumb, Bertha. What do you want? I haven't done a thing to hurt you."

"Oh yeah?" Now she starts to shriek, and the others smirk. "I want you to get the hell out of here, and I'm going to make sure you go. How's that, Miss Fancy Lady?"

"If this is about your husband, I am not going to budge." Sophie holds the reins taut. "You know better than anyone else what he is. You aren't going to change him by coming after me. Come on, Bertha. Let's talk this out. This isn't about you and me." The horse is wary. A few drops of rain pelt his mane and neck.

With both feet flat, Bertha seems fixed to the spot, as though she is unsure what to do next. For a brief moment, Sophie thinks that the woman is going to be sensible. Perhaps Bertha did not expect Sophie to stand her ground. She expected her to run, especially since she had her little army behind her. Sophie thinks maybe the two women can talk out what is standing between them.

Without taking another step, Bertha suddenly leans over and scoops up a rock. She is so quick about it, she doesn't give Sophie time to dodge. Her powerful arm flings it squarely at Sophie. She hears and feels the crack against her skull, and she emits a horrid scream. As if this is their signal to act, the women charge at Sophie and yank her off the Appaloosa. The terrified horse screeches and rises up on his back legs. Frantically, he punches at the air with his front hooves, connecting with the face of one of the women. She screams, as does the Appaloosa. Then into the darkness he bolts toward town, his reins flying behind him.

The rain is coming faster now, and Sophie's face is wet from tears and the sky. She holds her hand to her right ear, which is in excruciating pain. As the blows and kicks come, she wraps her arms around her head and sobs. The ground turns slippery as ice, and it is difficult for the women to strike with precision. Each time she gets hit, the ear pain disappears briefly. She protects her head, and she tries to avoid the punches by jerking and twisting her body, while at the same time kicking her legs wildly at her attackers. "You're not going to make me leave, Bertha," she screams between the sobs. "I'm not Wilma Waters." She's amazed to hear herself sound so fierce. "You hear me?" She does not notice that the rain has eased up, but suddenly the blows stop coming. She wonders how long it has been, and if she fainted. Someone is speaking.

"Well, goll dang it, Bertha. What the heck is going on here?" Sophie is not sure if she is dreaming. Maybe she passed out, or maybe she was having a nightmare. Except there is this terrible pain in her ear, and the man's voice, although it sounds so faraway, made the blows stop.

"You stay out of this, Mr. Clawson," Bertha says.

"Now, Bertha. You know I can't do that. What have you gone and done to this poor girl here? Shame on you, Bertha. And shame on you other ladies. Now, go on. Get on home to your husbands." The rain has stopped now.

"Mind your own business." Bertha's hands are on her hips again. Mr. Clawson is on his horse, rain still dripping off his hat. He's trailing Sophie's Appaloosa behind him. He is not sure whether Bertha is in a foul enough temper to lunge out at him. But the other women have faded into the shadows of the night.

"Bertha, you and me both know that this girl don't have nothing to do with how that lout of a husband treats you. You're just trying to get back at him. Ain't you? You didn't have no call to hurt this girl, though."

"What do you know about it? She put him up to it."

"You know that just ain't true, don't you?"

"No." Bertha growls, then stifles a wail that is long overdue and unexpected. Not one person, until now, has confirmed to her face the truth of what she has had to endure. That a man is saying it straight out to her catches her off her guard. She is sweaty and filthy from the mud. Her heart is pounding from the exertion.

"Bertha? You got a son of a bitch for a husband. There ain't no getting around that fact. But what you going to do? Beat up every girl he looks at? You gotta find another way, Bertha. Don't you know that? This ain't doing nobody no good."

"I don't know," Bertha murmurs. Sophie, still lying on the ground, is groaning and writhing. Out of nowhere, Bertha lets out a piercing wail pitiful as a wounded animal. She falls to her knees right next to Sophie and howls. Sophie has her ears covered but the screams are unbearable in her good ear. In the other, the noise is muffled, and sounds like a coyote crying a ridge or two away. In spite of the overwhelming pain, she wishes she had the strength to reach out to Bertha.

Mr. Clawson now has one hand on Sophie, trying to comfort her, and the other over Bertha's shoulder. Sophie is moaning, and Bertha is wailing, and Mr. Clawson, between the two, mumbles, "Lordy me. Lordy me." For a moment he remains there and is silent.

"What we need right now, ladies, is Mirna. Right now. Bertha, you're gonna be all right. Come on, now, and get up, old girl. I need your help. Time's a wastin'."

"Listen, now. You listening to me, Bertha? You help me get that girl up on her horse. We're taking her to Mirna. She'll fix her up. What in the hell did you do to her?"

The two of them do not see Pip arrive. He's pattered over to Sophie and is gently licking her head. With his forepaw on her chest, he comforts her and tries to stop her writhing. She puts a hand on his head and whispers, "Hello there, old Pip. We're going to be fine, now. Just fine." And then she passes out.

"By God, Bertha. Come on. You ain't a mean woman by nature. I can sure see that now. Let's get her on home now."

❧

Felix practices his mounting and dismounting on the Appaloosa in Mirna's yard. "By gum. I think you got it now, young man," Mr. Clawson encourages him. "Go ahead. Let's take him out on the road."

Mrs. Andersson walks into the yard just as they turn to leave. "Sure enough, she's bringing another pie or somethin' tasty for the womenfolk," Mr. Clawson says. "You gonna make them ladies in there fat, Mrs. Andersson."

"I hope so. How's Sophie doing today?"

"Well, with her mama and my Mirna looking after her, she's going to come out all right. That little girl is a fighter, that's for sure. Ain't that so, young fellow?"

"I sure hope so, Mr. Clawson. I sure do hope so. She's anxious to get out of bed and start writing the stories she hasn't gotten to out here. She says she's just getting started."

"Yep. She's gonna come out all right, Mrs. Andersson," Mr. Clawson yells over his shoulder, as the two mounted horsemen start up the road, with Pip running at their heels.

Nora

She Takes A Chance

I am sixty years old…I am active yet and more active than most younger women, so please think of me as physically able to endure. I have the courage and determination, and I am sure if any other lone woman can do it, I can too.

From *Montana Women Homesteaders: A Field of One's Own*

"Oh my God, it hurts!" Sprawled in a gully because her mare kicked up its hindquarters and sent her flying through the air like a rag doll, Nora clenches her teeth. She stifles a scream and grips a clump of early spring grasses to distract herself from the pain. The tears streaming into her ear do no earthly good, she chides herself, and if she were not in such terrible pain, she would insist, as she does with her pupils in Lewistown, that she take deep breaths and settle down.

Maggie, her generally reliable horse, is nonchalant above her at the road's edge, masticating fresh clumps of slender yellow-green grass, showing no remorse. "You despicable beast!" Nora cries out. She can see only the top of Maggie's head. "Well, I'm still conscious. I could be dead."

Despite the searing pain, she has a flash of belated empathy for the poor young lady over near Miles City who died when a horse kicked her in the head. She read about it in the *Montana News* just last week. Nausea is rising in her throat now from the blow, and she feels—and hopes—she is going to pass out, because the distress is agonizing. A bone protrudes just above her high-top shoes. If she doesn't stay awake, perhaps no one will find her. As long as she is alert, she can cry out if she hears horses coming. She fears that the mare may wander off to better feeding grounds, where someone will spot the horse and empty saddle and start a search there, in the wrong place! Wiping her shoulder against her cheek, she dries the tears collecting in a puddle at her neck. This current predicament is just one too many. She is furious and wants to scream from both the torment and her anger. How will she manage now, trying to get about on a broken leg? That is, *if* they find her before it's too late. There's her teaching job and her homestead. Without her salary, she will not be able to pay to have her crops put in and harvested.

"You must stay awake! You are in a pickle barrel of trouble now, Nora." Even through her moans, she reproaches herself for not preventing the accident. She blames it on her nonstop litany, the near-constant self-dialogue that first started during the winter when she had too little to keep her mind occupied beyond correcting school papers. If she had been paying attention, she would have spied the snake stretched out halfway across the road before Maggie did. The mare isn't seeing any too well anymore.

The nausea is coming in waves, and she has to act quickly. She forces herself to sit up and pulls at the edges of her skirt. She tears strips of cloth to tie around the leg, one above and one below the break to stabilize it. She isn't able to pull her boot off, so she wraps the second piece around it at the ankle. The nausea eases a bit. The blood is soaking into her skirt. If it were midsummer, she could use yarrow leaves—if some plants were nearby—to stop the oozing.

Only moments before, Nora had been nagging the horse, commanding her to lift her ancient hooves and get fired up. She had told her to stop dragging her tail and suggested that she pretend she was a young filly once again out for an adventure. Then she chuckled and said she would do the same.

They had been headed toward town and the schoolhouse. It was a fine day, and the wind was for once at peace with itself. She was staring off dreamily at the fresh green fields, mindful that she didn't have to hold down the top of her bonnet to keep it from flying off. She noticed that the buttercups had popped out just since yesterday. Against the morning sun, their bold gold glittered like a pretty woman who, even when demure, does not go unnoticed.

Interspersed in her horse monologue was the argument she was formulating to present to Jessie Mae. She was not confident yet that she had fully persuaded her granddaughter to move out to Montana to be her companion so she wouldn't have to pack up and leave, as so many of the others had. Where does an old lady go when she doesn't have a man anymore and there is no other place to go? Back to her daughter and son-in-law in Ohio?

The thought of having to move in with her daughter nearly sent her into a chilly ague. She knew herself well enough after all these years that if she were back there with Eliza, she would stick her nose in and tell her to get herself a backbone. Ralph and she would probably both toss Nora out on her ear. No, she was where she needed to be: on her own out there for as long as her heart held out and the elements didn't take her.

Lord knows she'd never get another man. One of them in a woman's lifetime was probably already one too many. Yet she'd been eyeballed by Old Man Perkins during the winter when she was living in town. They met at a dance at the schoolhouse; he was playing the fiddle, and she was serving punch.

Mrs. Andersson brought him over to the table and said, "Nora, I don't believe you've met Mr. Perkins. He asked me to introduce him."

He winked at her after Mrs. Andersson moved on. "Seems Mrs. Andersson about knows everyone around here, don't she?"

She asked, "Would you like some punch, Mr. Perkins?"

He told her he regretted he had to tap his foot and play tunes for the crowd, because otherwise he'd be right happy to take a turn with her. "Just call me Hank, by the way," he had said.

"Anybody play that piano there?" He nodded toward the upright in a corner of the room.

She said she gave it a try now and again. It wasn't proper to point out she had been classically trained and could keep a tempo at which not even Mozart would scoff.

Hank showed up at the schoolhouse one day during lunchtime. She was embarrassed, mainly because the children were present, and also because it had been many years since anyone had demonstrated an affectionate interest.

He came another time, when the children already had gone home, and brought his violin. He wanted to do duets, of all things. He folded himself into one of the children's desk chairs, and she played Franz Liszt's "Liebestraum" for him. He hummed parts of it, tapping his fingers, and said he had heard the piece somewhere before. She wished the piano were not so out of tune. She wished she would have thought to play a livelier piece like a sonata.

Then it was his turn. The melancholy tale of "Barbary Ellen," though mournful, was pleasing to her ear. She did not recognize the song and didn't know it came to the Appalachians by way of England, but she liked that it repeated itself so she could catch its melody. In plucky fashion, after he had finished, she picked the tune out on the piano with one finger. Oh, Hank liked that! He told her he was sure they could make music together, and he ordered some duets from a catalog, but that didn't work out because he could not read a note.

For a time, she felt like she was twenty-one again and kicking up her heels to impress that Dutchman who had stolen her heart at a barn dance a lifetime ago. Oh, the Dutchman had liked her. Right from the start. Tumbled through the barn door, nearly falling flat on his face in front of her because he was looking at her and not watching where he put his feet. Those were hopeful days. She thought she must have been a looker, the way those boys fluttered around her, and her knocking them back like they were flies. She had yearned to go on the stage, singing and acting. She thought she was good at it, too. Better maybe than Lillian Russell. But Mother would not permit it. Young girls from decent homes didn't display themselves in public for all the world (and particularly men) to see. Later—but that was after she had married the Dutchman—she wanted to be a writer. Not like Browning. No, she only read her recently because she had nearly worn out the George Eliot books, and that too-prim Jane Austen. Next on her list were the gloomy Brontës, and following that, the even broodier Thomas Hardy, but only on summer evenings, or else she would get dragged down by both them and the harsh winter.

She was planning a further strategy for Jessie Mae as she and Maggie ambled on. The horse moved at her own pace, and they were two miles from town, which was why she let her thoughts rush like water through a sieve. She had rebuked herself and Maggie a mile back about this particular habit, but both she and the horse had ignored her admonishment. "Nora, you are carrying on. You've barely gotten your eggs and potatoes eaten and your horse saddled. Too early in the day to start with worries. Once you start this dirge you know well and good how the rest of the day will go." She had no premonition, however, that she was going to end up in a ditch with not a soul around to help her.

She reproved herself for babbling. She was beginning to sound like the old rover preacher, Holmquist. He went around on his prehistoric mule, muttering, "Blessed redeemer" at about the beginning or end of every sentence, and nobody listening to him. "Lord knows that is a great deal too many blesseds of anything for my liking. This wind makes me want to rumble 'blessed something' myself when it doesn't let up."

The sun was glistening on Maggie's tawny neck, and its brightness cautioned Nora against dawdling any longer; the day was moving ahead, and they needed to step up their speed. She would have been quite happy not to have to lead some dense heads today who didn't want to learn arithmetic any more than she wanted to teach it. Especially on such a glorious day.

"Let's get a move on here. How am I going to make any headway at this pace? You're as stubborn, I swear, Maggie, as that old Dutchman. I could never get him to agree to go in the same direction I wanted to go. We must get to the schoolhouse ahead of those children. We must always set the example. Otherwise the alert ones with sharp minds and sharper tongues will be so tiresome. Timeliness, Maggie— they'll remind me for the rest of the year. I know, I know, you just yearn to turn your rump right around and make a beeline back to your hay and the comfort of the barn."

Nora sighed. She'd like a little of that comfort herself, truth be told. Sit in her rocker for the day, inside her tar-paper shack, listening to the crickets serenading her inside the walls with a noisy melody, her lumpy, warm quilt over her knees, and a small glass of whiskey at her elbow. Oh, yes! Wouldn't she like to take a sip every ten pages while she read Elizabeth Barrett Browning's letters? "Lordy, she was a romantic girl, wasn't she? City born and bred. She wouldn't have lasted long in Lewistown, Montana."

She would write another letter today to Jessie Mae and describe Montana just as the Northern Pacific Railroad did in their newspaper ads. Those Northern Pacific Railroad newspaper ads—lies!—lured gullible fools out to Montana for free land to homestead, more than likely assuming they were all dumb as asses. Oh, didn't they paint a very rosy picture of how pleasant the weather was here? A most moderate climate. They would be living in clover.

That rosy picture of pleasant weather made the state sound like paradise. The technique had worked on her and other homesteaders, and Nora wasn't going to ruin her chance of convincing Jessie Mae to move out here by telling her about the angry winds that whipped through the wheat fields. Or the rolls of dust that screened the sun off and made it look like the moon was standing in the middle of the day. Many times she had wondered if the wind might whip her own head off her shoulders. Nora grumbled, "Somehow those ads managed to overlook this incessant wind, as though it wasn't worth mentioning."

It was most agreeable that the day was turning out to be so splendid and calm. She wouldn't be deceiving Jessie Mae today to describe this place with only positive adjectives. If Jessie Mae didn't come—Nora dared not be too hopeful— she could end up being blue and down in the dumps for a good long time.

She and the mare were becoming intoxicated by the unexpected day's warmth. Yet even on such a nice day, she had a nagging bee buzzing around her bonnet about the future and the notion that only trouble and woes lay ahead. "Mother used to tell me, 'Nora, you need to stop worrying all the time. Never borrow trouble till trouble bothers you.' She said I never seemed to get enough worrying done. Told me she had not seen anything like me in her life."

The Lord knew that she wanted to be ready for any crazy wildcat that might jump out of the bushes and chase away her still-small hope that things would turn out all right. But the day was too lovely to dwell on uncertainty. There were tiny purple flowers all around. She hadn't seen anything like them before. They certainly didn't grow in Ohio.

Oh, those old ladies back in Ohio and the sights they were missing. "I can just hear those wise ones who stayed back there." She chuckled. "They'd have a good laugh, wouldn't they? 'Old Nora, what a fool she was,' they'd cluck if they could see me most days now, skirt and petticoat flying high above my waist like kites; if they were not firmly attached to me, they would soar right up to the heavens. Probably take me with them, but I am not ready yet"—she chuckled again—"to meet my Maker. 'You'd think a woman her age…she was at least sixty, wasn't she, by the time she packed up and left?'"

They probably said she never did have good sense. If that were the case, they were well rid of her, because if the wind didn't topple her off the aging nag sooner or later, smashing her brains in on a boulder like that young schoolteacher over east, or a blizzard didn't ambush her and smother her out on the flats this winter, or her stove didn't blow up because she threw too much coal in it to keep out the minus-forty-degree chill like the one that showed up the night before last Christmas, she guessed she'd be lucky.

To call temperatures that dropped below zero a *chill* was utter nonsense. It was ironic, at best. Worse yet, sadistic. As a woman who appreciated literature, she determined that there was a very limited choice of words available to describe the earthly torments that appeared without warning. "If none of those things get me, I am sure a rattlesnake will finish me off, or I'll die of thirst because that young Clay who transports my water three miles every two weeks fails to show up, or I'll starve because the rain won't come, and the fields will dry up for good this summer."

She just hoped Jessie Mae decided to board that train sometime soon and didn't change her mind and decide that, after all, she was going to marry that knuckleheaded bricklayer boy she'd known all her life, who couldn't read a book to save his soul. He was no match for her smart and vivacious granddaughter. She was too lively to settle down and live life behind a picket fence like her mother, with a screened-in porch and a know-it-all husband. Jessie Mae could take right over the teaching when she arrived. If she needed Nora's help to get adjusted to the hardy children, most of them smarter than many a grown man and woman, she would be happy to point the way.

"Those children are going to be peeking out the windows soon, Maggie, keeping their fingers crossed in hopes I won't come. Who doesn't want a reprieve from calculating prices or deciding how many commas to put in sentences, and where to fit them all? Especially when there are swings and softball beckoning them."

There is little shade in the ravine, and the sun is already intense. The dew that clung to the grasses when the mare threw her has evaporated. She is not sure how much time has passed. She retched after she bound up her leg then slipped into a peaceful torpor. The heat of the sun awakens her, boring through the fabric of her dress. She feels the beads of sweat in her hair, although the brim of her bonnet covers most of her face, and her dress has long sleeves. It must be almost noon. The horse is no longer in her view. She likely drifted off when she got thirsty. Nora's throat is parched, and the nausea is coming again. She has to try to pull herself up out of there.

Just before the accident occurred, she had been about to explain to the mare that if the sun was going to be so brazen, instilling hope and radiating heat, they would need to be watchful for snakes basking in its warm rays. By the time she actually saw the monstrous reptile stretched over the road, she did not have time to cry, "Watch out, Maggie!" before the horse stumbled over it and panicked. She sent Nora flying. If her leg hadn't collided with the rock on the way down, it would not look like a stick caught above her boot. She wasn't one to crumble like an empty eggshell.

Recently she had been telling herself she deserved a good pat on the back for getting through the tough winter. Well, she hadn't stayed out in her shanty during the worst of it, but still she had to muscle the feed for her mare. How many women her age could manage the bales of hay as she had? She was grateful for the children who brought fuel in the evenings to the place she rented in town. When most of the snow had disappeared, she moved back out to the shack. Daylight was lasting now until after she washed up the supper things.

She wasn't sure that she wasn't an old goose, she told Maggie. She could have stayed in Ohio and shriveled up like an acorn squash after the frost. "I could have been in town near that daughter of mine and that husband of hers!" But when she pictured Ralph's face, she stopped short. Whenever she thought of him, she found it necessary to counsel herself that he wasn't worth getting worked up over.

She reminded herself to be grateful she wasn't in the kind of straits her neighbor Bertha Wilcox was in. Well, if she was to put a fine point on it, in some ways she and Bertha shared a similar history. Oh, the Dutchman caused her grief for sure. At this ripe age, she perhaps could begin to see that he was not able to keep his distance—or his hands—from women with thick and healthy hair. She knew without one ounce of doubt that he had loved her, for all his wandering. "Is it possible, do you think, Maggie, to conclude that he was as much tormented as I by his actions?" She felt sorry for poor Bertha, though. Mr. Wilcox did not seem to give any thought to her. It was no surprise she took her anger out on pretty little Sophie. It was a wonder the woman could hold her head up after she beat the girl up so badly. It was dreadful to consider what would have happened if Mr. Clawson had not come along at the right moment.

"But if it is men we are talking about, Maggie"—her voice

was dreamy and distant like the flax gently waving on a hillock—"since Hank Perkins has apparently disappeared to who knows where, I have to say I am a bit curious about little Frankie's grandfather. I should not be saying this, should I? Honestly, a woman my age! But he is a funny character, and he makes me laugh. If I was of a mind to marry again, he'd have me quicker than a hawk swooping down on a field mouse."

It was that peculiar way he entertained the kids when he came to walk Frankie home after school. The children could not wait to see him limping up the road. "Mr. Hawthorne, Mr. Hawthorne, show us your short leg, please," they'd plead.

You'd have to wonder how they could be excited to see the same spectacle day after day, but they were. "Odd thing is, I look forward to it as much as the kids and laugh at it every time, too. Him standing by my desk, holding onto its edge with one hand and smiling over at me like he is doing it for my benefit while he balances on his long good leg and swings the short one back and forth. All the kids ask him if it is a trick, and he just grins at them. They ask Frankie, too, and he shrugs his shoulders, but little Frankie is so proud of his grandfather. He takes his hand after they walk out of the schoolyard."

Poor Mr. Hawthorne. He had such good humor for someone who lost his wife not more than a year before. If the old Dutchman had been as good a nurse as Mr. Hawthorne, Nora wouldn't have wanted to give up being tended to with calm and patient care. But that was only speculation, since the old Dutchman would no more be a faithful nurse than he was a faithful man.

Nora hoped that she wouldn't walk into that schoolhouse to find a letter from Jessie Mae telling her she had decided to marry that young man. She wanted her to do what she hadn't done when she was young. "I don't want her to get old before she sets out on her own and samples adventure and independence. When I prove up, I can pass my land on to her. She can own it someday—as long as she doesn't lose her heart to some cowpoke and marry him. Why are women at the mercy of men's rules?"

She was in sympathy with those women up in Canada who weren't allowed to become homesteaders. They had to move down to the States to get that chance. "We are constrained by our sex, Maggie, but thank goodness those politicians in Washington, DC, had enough sense to vote in favor of women homesteaders. I cannot imagine where I would be if that wasn't so."

She wondered how much common sense those congressmen had, however, when they allowed an eighty-year-old woman up near Glasgow to take up a homestead. That remarkable lady must have been someone's grandmother! Or auntie, or cousin. It defied logic to think of the aged woman stooped over a well, pulling up a bucket of water, or out in the yard on her way to the barn to feed animals in a katabatic wind that could topple her over without any compassion for her age. Someone must have built a shack for her, put in her fields, and planted trees. Nora was nearly twenty years younger, and she already needed a good deal of outside help for the physical tasks.

And no one spoke about the emotional ups and downs, either. The nearest anyone came to doing so was to discuss the weather, letting it take the brunt for blue moods and hostile feelings. It was hard enough to carry around a mountain of one's own worries. Unless you were Mrs. Andersson, who just never seemed to have any cares of her own. Nora had lugged her own heavy heart over to that lady on especially gloomy occasions and come away uplifted, for Mrs. Andersson found just the right thing to say. Her words were a bridge that quietly moved troubles over a raging stream. You didn't want to let Mrs. Andersson down once she had consoled you.

She feels light-headed. She can't slow the nystagmic motion in her eyes. It is from the exertion of maneuvering through boulders while dragging her damaged leg behind, and trying not to knock it against anything or catch the bone on a bush. She has pulled herself partway up the ravine and has not heard anyone pass along the road. She cannot hear if Maggie is still nearby. She must reserve her strength so she can call out. When she determined she would climb out, she first whispered a sincere prayer to not put her hand in a nest of rattlers. She vomits again, and everything goes dark.

The Dutchman often told Nora she was unusual. He did not say it in a derisive way. "Norie"—he'd puff up with pride—"you are never boring. No, sir. If I live to be a hundred, you will always surprise me." That didn't keep him from wandering, though. It was in his nature. If he were still alive and scanning this horizon, his eyes squinting to make things out at a distance, he would surely say, "There is not a woman for very many miles who has your education and upbringing, Norie." It was because of her mother, always pushing her to be the best. She said she didn't want Nora to end up in a dead end. Maybe that was why Nora was not satisfied, not content to live her final years in surroundings that knew her like she knew the veins on the top of her hands. "Maybe that is why I left my home, my daughter and granddaughter, and that familiar world. I wish I really knew why I left it all. There seem to be many whys on the road today.

"Maybe I was a cantankerous old fool. I moved out here to prove I am not an old woman yet, and I was not going to let that Ralph put me out to pasture. And I'm doing the same for you, Maggie, my girl, although I think you would be delighted if I gave up on you and let you have your way. Maybe you and I should both turn around—no, no, not back to the barn." Wouldn't it be sensible to give in to defeat and climb aboard that train going back East? To forgive Ralph for being Ralph, so she could die near her daughter, Eliza, someday, probably sooner than later? "Oh, I miss her so. When I receive a letter—and there are never enough of them—I cannot determine if I am in more distress holding onto paper she has written on in her own hand or having to wait so long between letters."

Eliza should have had better sense twenty years ago than to marry that penny-pinching Ralph. Maybe it was Nora's fault. She wanted the girl to make up her own mind. "Didn't I do that with the Dutchman? No one told me any better. A person has to decide that kind of thing for themselves. Better leave that regret dying on the vine with the gourd.

"Oh, there are some days here I cannot forget. They are as

memorable as a mother taking her brand-new baby into her arms the first time. Like today!" Nora could not help but be in rapture about this unknowable and often-disturbing land. Sometimes, in the very early morning light, when she was on her way to the barn, a warm wave washed over her skin and hair, bathing her like Queen Bathsheba in fragrant oils so gentle, so exhilarating! And those rainbows of colors in an evening sky, shades that could not be real or even exist. Back in Ohio they would not believe her *if* she had words to describe the glory that filled the huge orange sky at the end of the day. She regretted that people she cared for should be missing out on the assets that nature gave to the sparsely settled land. Colors that even dreams could not create, and as elusive as dreams. They came and went so quickly, she was reluctant to believe she experienced them. "Like a thief in the night. Thief in the night," she whispered.

"That other life back in Ohio doesn't leave me alone some days. It haunts me and won't leave me in peace. I cannot look back without regret. I stumble over these feet. Old as I am, you'd think I would have found it in my heart to be kinder to those I left behind." She had come to it late, discovering her untamed streak among the wild surroundings, and often she did not like what she had come to know about herself. She asked the horse and herself why the salt of life had not put enough seasoning over her soul before now so she could be a savory dish to bring to the table. "Many is the time I have been a stubborn woman hauling around a basketful of grudges like those meaty potatoes I dug out of my garden late last summer. I think back to that life, and I shake my head at—what can you call it other than arrogance?" She never wanted for comforts there, even after the Dutchman died.

She did not have to do men's work out of doors, coaxing things to grow with all her back and sweat locked into it as she had to do now. She hired out the hardest work with the money she earned at the school. It didn't go that far, a hundred dollars every month, but if her wheat held on this year, she could make a profit between that and the flax. "If I do, I will put in a well so my Jessie Mae and I can have water close by." She wouldn't want her granddaughter to have to adapt to surviving on the meager portions of water she rationed between Clay's deliveries.

She had leaped—it was true—at the idea of moving out West, an impressionable old fool tempted by the enticing newspaper ads. To this day she looked into that mirror in her tiny parlor, and a furrowed face looked back with those uneven and wandering lines, not anything like her straight wheat fields. *Who is this with such unruly gray hair?* And oh, that sweet Eliza, the black cloud of her face when Nora had told her she had packed up and bought a ticket out here. The poor girl was as distressed as a newborn goat kid searching for its nanny. As for Ralph, as soon as his accounting brain heard the news, he was tallying dollars and nickels, calculating what her fool adventure would cost, predicting in his eternal certainty that she would go bankrupt in a year or so, and she would have to be retrieved by him—God forbid—in the end.

The most satisfying thing was that for two years she hadn't seen Ralph's face—yet. But she missed her Eliza so, her countenance as warm and forgiving as the few giant sunflowers Nora encouraged with devotion and dedication in her garden. They brought her dear girl closer during the summer. That must be why she nurtured them so. When winter came, she could not seem to remember what Eliza looked like. The only image that appeared was of her as a toddler running across the wood floor in their parlor and into Nora's arms. The Dutchman was jolly, his pipe smoke flavoring the air, Eliza giggling, her little legs not yet steady under her. "Oh Lordy, Maggie, it will help to have Jessie Mae here. She doesn't bring Eliza to me, but thank goodness I can't see Ralph in her features either!"

The sun has shifted to the other side of the ravine, and because she is in shadow, the coolness rouses her, and she shivers. Her throat is parched. The leg is numb, and she feels terribly exhausted. She does not have enough strength to pull herself up any farther but knows she will most certainly die if she doesn't try. She has a terrifying idea of someone finding her while she is still alive but being too late to save the leg.

As she and the mare ambled toward town, she marveled at the wildflowers coming on. Only a few days earlier, the ground had been hard and silent. Now it was talking, practically screaming at her to look and enjoy it. The plants leaned their faces toward the sun boldly defying the threat of not yet finished foul weather. "Oh no, you don't, you conniving animal! You are not going to start nibbling grass. Trying to take advantage of me as soon as my mind starts to wander." The wild flax swished and swayed among the grasses, partners recently discovering each other at a dance. She was violet, he a brassy green. "Would you look at that, Maggie? They're dancing like we did once," she sighed remembering the waltzes with the Dutchman. The fractious gusts were gone for the moment, replaced by a zephyr. "The wind is teasing us, but we know better, don't we, Maggie? We won't let it make fools of us any longer.

"Perhaps that's what drove me out West—oh, I am going on this morning." She wished the reason could be elevated. If only she could attribute the decision to an intellectual curiosity that needed satisfying. "The truth is I had the silly notion there was more air to breathe out here." That sounded preposterous, probably even to the old horse that had walked and labored on this earth for too many years. Air is air anywhere. "Was it that I was *blessed*—there you go again with that overworked word, Nora—with too many opportunities in the course of a life?"

That sounded decidedly contradictory. Of course it did. Why would she have ventured out here when she had everything she wanted? For someone untouched by poverty or hunger or lack of education, who never knew want, were those very privileges accompanied by their own liabilities? It was absurd. She wanted to blame her doubts and questions on the weather, or the landscape, or the physical difficulties, but how could she? More likely the blame lay in the length of time it took for an old horse to get her to school, and an open expanse that beckoned her, like the finger of God pointing her to go inward.

"If I told Ralph that it was *because* I had lived a privileged life and that drew me out to Montana, he would dismiss me with a snort and that awful condescending laugh of his." She grimaced and imagined him peering inside his sleeve to pull out one of his undefeatable arguments. The colossal choice to move was rash she realized now that she had distance and time to fully review it. She had to admit she jumped without looking at the consequences. One fine, brilliant morning in Ohio, when the rays of sun bounced off a foot of snow forcing her to shield her eyes from their power, her mind became clear. It revealed one stark fact that engaged and propelled her. *"I was acting like I was alive without being alive!"* she enlightened Maggie. She had grown up with all the advantages from money to a very good education, and it took one flash of clarity for them to gag her like a too-large chunk of meat that she had been trying for far too long to swallow. She was accustomed to a comfortable existence. She assumed that she deserved it or it would not have been given. She was not ignorant of how people lived who did not have her advantages, but they were not her concern. If God had meant for them to be well-off he would have provided. The day the sun shone on that snow she pictured a wagon with everyone she knew in it. They had been riding together all along in the same direction without her knowing it, in the wagon of life, but on wheels of odd sizes, with the wobble and tilt more noticeable for those who traveled on the smaller ones.

The children here, some so poor they came to school with rags wrapped round their feet, should have the chance to have an education. Their parents had to make a sometimes tough choice of either sending their kids to school or keeping them on the homestead to do the chores. Between them and the ever-present incalculable weather, which was often frightening, and the work and difficulties that swallowed her up some days, she felt the mask had been pulled off her old face. Her eyes once took a straight-ahead view because they could.

The reverie billowed inside her like her skirt did in the wind.

It was as insidious as a three-day battle she'd had with the wind squealing through her hut, wearing a kerchief over her mouth and nose to keep the dust from choking the air out of her, and having to either swallow grit or spit it out. She felt tired. She was tired of herself, tired of listening to her repetitions. "Dare I say it, Maggie? Tired of breathing."

"Now, Maggie, you have to listen to me—or do you?" She chuckled. "About that business of forgiving—well, Ralph, of all people. Don't come back and remind me about it when I start going off on another of my rants. I just can't get over Ralph taking my Eliza from me. But that was so long ago—can I really still be holding onto that?" The day they ran off, the Dutchman had tried to quiet her down, but she wouldn't listen to him. She glared at him. "I told him that the only thing that was mine was stolen from me. He said, "'You always have me, Nora—for all eternity.'"

"Can you just imagine that, Maggie? I laughed in his face, but I felt like spitting in it."

She had started to wonder if by making her claim she had been looking for a way to replace the emptiness she felt about Eliza leaving her. If that was so, then the gossips back in Ohio may have assessed her correctly. If that was the case, she was worse than a child throwing herself on the floor in a pout over a toy. "I'm grinding the wheat too fine today, Maggie."

Before the Dutchman ever came along, she was so sure of herself. He caused her a great deal of grief in his lifetime, but she had her ways of getting back at him later on, when she finally got it through her head that arguing with him was not going to change him and make him into the perfect human being she thought she had married. A fury still shook through her when she let herself dwell on it. "Who keeps paying the price for that if it's not me? It is an expensive purchase that doesn't stop costing." He was not there to rail against. She had stopped saying she loved him, kept living with him, and acted for all her might like she hated him. "I did not let him get any closer than a rattler sunning itself across the path on a warm day." If she turned around and looked back on all of it, she would have to say that she was as bitter as red wine gone sour. But when she had been young, and someone had crossed her, and she was in pain because she was not going in the direction she hoped to be—well, there was no relief at all from that kind of misery.

"I thought coming out here would change me. If I had land of my own where no one but me had a say in what I was doing, I could be happy."

She liked to think she was heroic. That she made the decision to be a part of a history that surely would go down in the annals of America's early days. If a man could come West and settle this land in an arm wrestle of wills against nature, to bend it like hot iron his way, then a lone woman could do the same. She imagined she would have a most productive homestead and even envisioned newspaper headlines back in Ohio, where Ralph would read about her success and would have to change his view that his mother-in-law was befuddled or childish. Stories of her great adventure would highlight the fact that instead of sitting on the front porch waiting for great-grandchildren to show up, she was making her share of history.

Thus far she had endured fickle temperatures that toyed with and teased the mind. Her hands, once soft as kid leather, felt like burlap. The volume of hair that used to be coiled in a French twist and protected by a green velvet hat and pheasant feather, sat like a gray cow patty on top of her head. In the end, the decision to leave Ohio had proven to be a move to stave off that loneliness that had not lifted since Eliza married. When the Dutchman passed on, there was little enough in Ohio to keep her there. "If Jessie Mae comes, as she has promised, I will be content. I promise myself that. I will not grumble or talk myself silly," she promised. She mocked herself for decisions which seemed as fruitless as trying to tie a knot with only one end of a rope.

If she had gone on the stage when she was young, a longing she had stored but neglected in the cellar of her mind all these years, she would have become someone important. She would have had purpose along with fame. She had not been content with the Dutchman's love. It did not measure up to what she had expected. Other women closed their eyes to their husbands' excesses, but no, not her. They learned to wrap up their heartache in lace making or tatting, and tying threads into tiny knots. They tied off what couldn't be fixed. Yes, she did know how much he loved her. But disappointment was eating, eating, eating inside her, agitating and fussing and not ever filling her up. "Maggie, for all that gnawing away inside me, I am ravenous as a pig at the trough that never gets its fill, no matter how many times it dips its head in the swill."

She could boast that she was quite fit for one who had passed her sixtieth year. "I venture to say there is not more than one in ten women my age willing enough, or maybe stupid

89

enough, to start a homestead." She let out a dismissive laugh.

Those comfortable women she had left behind on broad porches in Ohio would express more colorful words than they had heard in a lifetime if they had to break up sod for a garden or haul buckets of water, or shovel hay twice a day. If you put them together to make one human being, there wouldn't be enough gumption from the mix for one of them to leave behind family and a home. She would have liked to brag about her spirit—but to whom?—and to say she was superior in some way, for that thought did tickle a familiar bone. "But it's been my pride, Maggie, driving me out of control like the horse of that reckless teacher." She shook her shoulders to brush off the notion of herself as a foolish girl who all these years had walked around in a woman's body.

"I wake up during many a night, remembering people who let me down over the years." She could not count the number of times she felt cheated out of her fair share of justice. To retrieve it, she had rebuffed people. "Yes, Maggie, I walked by them, and snubbed them. Even years after an offense if I saw them coming toward me, I reviewed their grievances."

The wind had gone to its cave while she rode toward town. She wanted to thank the Lord in the heavens above for the respite. She bet that even old preacher Holmquist and she could share a few blesseds on that. If it stayed as it was, it was going to be one of those Montana days that cannot be described in letters sent back home, because even with all the words in the dictionary, not a one of them could put it on a platter for Sunday dinner.

"Nora. Nora, can you hear me?" Someone is lifting her. Either it is evening, or she is losing her sight.

"Stop it! Oh, God, it hurts!"

"Sorry. We'll be very careful. We're going to make a spot on the ground until the wagon comes, Nora. Do you know who I am?"

Her head is spinning. "I'm so thirsty."

Someone hands her water.

"Nora, you've broken your leg."

She nods.

"Did you wrap that leg yourself?" His face is nearly touching hers, and she is bewildered from the pain of being moved. She doesn't know whether to yank his glasses off or kiss him in relief.

"Nora, do you recognize me?"

"Yes, yes." Of course she knows who he is. Everyone knows he is the young, fancy lawyer with that place next to Sophie's.

They wrap her in a blanket. She hears people around her whispering. They could be Bertha and Mrs. Andersson. She is not sure.

Felix speaks to her like she does with some of the slower children in class. "We had to pull you out of the ravine. They're bringing a wagon for you now."

"I'm so cold."

Someone comes with another blanket.

"Did you pull yourself out of there on that bad leg?" Bertha moves her gently as she wraps another blanket around her. She is able to manipulate the leg just enough to take the pressure off and ease the pain. Nora smiles weakly at her and falls into a sleep.

"You gave us a big scare, Miss Nora." Mr. Hawthorne is standing three feet away, holding his hat in front of him. "Little Frankie came running back home to tell me you hadn't made it to school, but your mare had. Did they tell you where they found your horse?"

The doctor's surgery is surprisingly cozy. There's a cheerful Tiffany lamp at her bedside, and the nurse brought her tea in a bone-china cup and saucer hand painted with bright daffodils. "I assume I have been here for several days." She sees that her leg is still attached, thank goodness, but at the moment she would like it to feel less intrusive.

"We had a search party out looking for you. We must have created quite a spectacle, all of us odds and ends on our horses not knowing where to look and poking around every bush and cranny. Nobody could believe that Felix with his bad eyesight would be the one to discover you, him with his fear of horses and all. But no one can argue that he found you, clutching at some grass by the edge of the road. You almost pulled yourself clear out of there. You are a very strong lady, Miss Nora."

"Maybe Sophie will marry Felix yet." She musters a small

smile.

"That wouldn't be a bad choice."

"How long *have* I been here, Mr. Hawthorne?"

"Three days now. Doc says you're lucky you didn't lose that leg. If you hadn't pulled yourself up to the road, it might have been several days before you got help, and if you hadn't wrapped the leg up, it might have been a different story. Now, he says, it will be good as the other one. Just a bit shorter." He laughs. "Between the two of us, we'll be able to put on a fine show for the children when you are ready to come back to school."

"Oh, dear. However will I manage now?" Oh, that embarrassing habit of hers. It is not Maggie she is talking to. She nearly jumps when Mr. Hawthorne responds to her.

"Don't you worry about a thing, Miss Nora. Sophie is taking over your duties at school. Look, I brought cards the children made for you."

"They did?"

"And Mr. Clawson has already plowed your fields. Says he'll plant in a week, and when you are feeling fit, he is going to drive you out to supervise what he's doing."

"Oh, Lordy," she whispers, wiping her eyes.

"Oh, and there's one more thing."

She straightens her back, expecting he's kept the bad news till the end. She clears her throat and hesitates, looking at him sideways. "And what is that, Mr. Hawthorne?"

"Well, Miss Nora, I'm wondering"—and he pauses to clear his throat—"when you are up and on your feet again, if I might start calling on you."

"Oh, Mr. Hawthorne." She blushes.

"Well, I hope that means yes. If it does, you better start calling me Sam. In the meantime, I can visit every day, and if you like, I'll read my favorite author to you."

"And who might that be?"

"Charles Dickens, of course." He laughs.

Mr. Hawthorne makes her smile at the most surprising times.

"By the way, I stopped off at the school to pick up a few things for you. I almost forgot—there was a letter from Ohio for you on your desk. I'll leave it here for you when you feel up to reading it."

Lizzie

The Reluctant One

The great majority of the women homesteaders…were from
the United States. Most were from Minnesota, with Iowa,
Wisconsin, North Dakota, and Illinois following. If they were
of "foreign" birth, most were from Norway, then Canada,
followed by Germany and Sweden, then England.

Sarah Carter, editor, *Montana Women Homesteaders*

Six inches of snow greets Lizzie at her door. The confection

swirls skirts of white powder onto her teetering wood step,
and she swishes her straw broom at it. Then she bobs her
head into the wind toward the barn where eight bawling cows
and two snorting sows are waiting for her. "I'm coming, for
goodness' sake."

She didn't forget, but she neglected to tie the laces on her
work boots before she left the shack, and as she negotiates
the drifts they flop like fish desperate to get back to water.

Snowflakes land on her eyelids and cheeks. She feels more than tastes the cold droplets on her tongue. She nearly falls over one of her laces into a snowbank halfway to the stable but catches herself. "You stupid girl!"

Her brother, Adam, without doubt, will be riding over from his neighboring homestead to check on her progress. If the animals are not tended to, he will start a row. She figures he will rant, and cringes at what he will say to her this morning. She despairs over his temper and anticipates what his next demand will be, even before he knows it himself, to stay a step ahead of him.

He is waiting for her at the barn. She doesn't notice him at once, astride his horse, for she is concentrating on her feet to avoid stepping on the laces. He is motionless as a military statue, his broad-brimmed hat sticking up like a white stovepipe. He shakes his head in disgust when he sees her coat flapping like giant wings, the buttons mismatched with their holes. The flakes spin off his hat brim, and he scowls at her untied boots. *She acts like a stubborn mule favoring a sore hoof.*

"How long were you gonna make them animals wait?" he chides, his clipped German ending on a sudden grace note. Her head snaps. *That blasted stove took too much time.* She couldn't get it to draw well and feared she would have to spend all day coaxing it to warm the shack. She glances back toward the house as though she might make a run to it. It's an impulsive reaction, but ridiculous since she has nowhere else to go.

She was fourteen when they'd arrived in North Dakota.

Adam, her eldest brother by fifteen years, along with his wife, Johanna, and their four young children, emigrated from their colony in Bessarabia. Papa had bribed Adam to take Lizzie. He sold off one of his milk cows to pay her passage and the food and room Adam would provide.

"I'm too old and crippled to go to America," Papa told Adam. His back had shriveled into the letter C, curving more each year from a blow he suffered by a rifle butt from his captain when he was a young man in the Russian army. Anti-German sentiment in Bessarabia was surging, and several nearby colonies had felt the brunt of that anger. Papa feared he could not keep Lizzie safe for much longer. He determined to send his favorite child away, knowing he would never see her again. Adam's narrow brow and gaunt brown features, prematurely frozen, lightened when Papa handed him a bag of gold coins.

Papa had not spared Adam from backbreaking work or oppressive discipline. When he was a child, Papa had been tyrannical, ordering his eldest son about with the severity he had experienced himself from his Russian commander. In Adam's adult life there had been two days he managed to produce a half smile: his wedding, and the birth of his first child.

"I won't baby her like you do," Adam declared.

"But watch out for her," Papa pleaded. He loathed entrusting Lizzie into Adam's care for he was not blind, nor was he senile. He might be a foolish old man, but he saw how Adam treated Johanna and their young children. If he were a fit young enough man himself, he would not have to beg for this favor and pray that his Lizzie would be treated well.

Lizzie, as the youngest and most prized of Papa's children, was the only one not married, and Papa could not sleep for fear she would be caught up in the violence from hostile Russian peasants. Only a half year earlier, the colony nearest theirs was raided. The mob burned golden fields of Turkey red wheat, kidnapped the small farm animals, and slaughtered the mules in front of the German men, armed with pitchforks, and standing frozen and dumb as their oxen and the gang coerced wives and daughters into potato cellars. Some of the women sneaked into bins and hid among the tubers and covered their ears against the screams of mothers, sisters, and friends until there were only whimpers, and finally, silence.

Papa would not permit talk about these brutal attacks to reach Lizzie's ears. When the family spoke of the *problem*, and it never was far from anyone's thinking, especially with the older sisters who had their own children to consider, voices turned low when Lizzie came around. Seated at Papa's wooden table, the glum faces alarmed Lizzie. "Papa, what are all of you talking about?" She was not a silly girl and the whispered conversations frightened her, but Papa replied, "This is not for you, *Liebchen.*"

In their tidy village, squat apple trees were budding pink blossoms when Adam's family bade their final good-byes. Lizzie sobbed in Papa's arms, wiping her tears and snot on his coarse shirt. "Why do I have to leave?" she begged. She gripped Papa until Adam pried her away and yelled, "Stop acting like a baby." Her siblings, the older sisters who envied Papa's partiality toward her, made faces behind Lizzie's back that Papa couldn't see. They often ridiculed her, to her face, told her she was dumb as an ox, and snickered if they could make her cry. *I will not miss them. I won't even remember them,* she resolved. Adam disentangled her from Papa's arms.

Papa fought back his own tears. "Little Skunk, it's for your own good," he said three times as if he was in church singing the chorus from the German hymnbook. He prayed that Adam would be considerate and not disclose the hardships to be faced by those left behind.

"She is a sensitive girl," he singsonged to Adam in the weeks before the departure. Surely if Adam understood her like he did, he would be gentle with her. Papa told him how Lizzie cried if a person in the village suffered. Hadn't she sat with the old man Keirleber when his wife died? Did Adam know that she stayed with the Hehn woman who could not get out of bed?

Lizzie searched her heart to fathom why Papa would abandon her, send her away to live in a foreign country with a brother who did not speak or look at her unless he required something. She found no satisfactory answer in her brooding. The muscles in her chest cavity ached from all the crying. She disguised her resentment, however, and reproved her rage toward Papa for pushing her away. She pitied the pain in his eyes and promised to do her best. She could not turn around to wave at him once the cart got underway.

Papa stood in the road staring after the cart although it had vanished off the horizon. One of the daughters called him to supper finally. He fell down on his knees and wept, right in the middle of the lane. "I couldn't tell her the real reason I sent her away," he wailed speaking to the tail end of the cart that was ten or more miles gone. The daughter patted his shoulder but he pushed her away.

"She's bright, Adam. She'll be a good teacher. See she gets the chance to go to school," Papa had advised following behind Adam as he carried one bundle, then another to the crowded cart once Johanna had them securely bound with thick cord at the necks. The colony teacher, Papa told Adam, the man classically trained and imported from Germany, had been very satisfied with Lizzie's grasp of the rules of grammar and math.

"She could write when she was just four," Papa boasted. At Papa's knees, after a supper of soup and *Dampfnudeln*, he had cheered her on with a piece of fruit each time she learned to write a letter of the alphabet in German, then Russian, using pencil stubs and scraps of paper collected from the school wastebasket. She loved climbing into his lap. Sometimes, during the lessons she slipped behind him and ran her fingers over his balding scalp. She adored him, liked the oily feel of his hair. Then, she'd kiss him on the back of his neck, and he'd laugh and pull her round to continue their study. He spoke the letters as he wrote them until Lizzie had the symbols memorized. She clutched the pencil with her chubby fist, attempting to imitate Papa. The teacher reported that Lizzie was a "bright and quick girl, obedient and a cheerful learner."

Adam would trade his favorite ox for ship passage once they arrived in Hamburg. On the journey there, the animal labored ahead of the cart piled with plump loaves of belongings, following rutted roads that became more tedious as the days went by. They passed vast open fields with moon-shaped snow patches neglected by the spring sun, lingering in thickets at the edges. From the Baltic harbor, they sailed aboard the *Patricia*, an uncertain freighter bound for America. Lizzie cried for seven days and nights.

Before they arrived in Hamburg, Adam made her get out of the cart on the third day. "You can walk until you stop your blubbering," he growled.

Aboard ship Adam repeated his order. "I am sick of your moaning about Papa. He can't hear your whining." She avoided him and found a private corner among the crates and barrels and continued to mourn for the father she knew she would not see again.

The waves battered them about and everyone turned a putrid shade of green and hung over the sides until there was nothing left in their stomachs. Even then the sickness did not subside. All, except Lizzie, and that was because, according to the captain, she did not take her eyes off the vanishing European horizon. Johanna wrapped herself in the ship's netting, all day and all night, and refused to come out until the captain finally took charge. Johanna at first refused to obey Adam, and he sent Lizzie to get her to come out since his barking had failed to dislodge her. Lizzie found it absurd that a grown woman should behave this way, but she spoke with tenderness, and in an even voice.

"Johanna," she said calmly, "will you come out? The children are asking for you." Lizzie spoke with respect as she had been taught to do with adults, but would not plead. Johanna ignored her.

When they disembarked in New York, they stumbled off the gangway and down narrow streets, where Lizzie's homesickness was swallowed up by the frenetic noises and strange tall buildings. While they had been in Hamburg, the towering buildings and the sky-reaching cathedrals had pulled her head back in search of the spires' tips. The people there were formal and dreary as the heavens in their drab clothing. The markets, unlike in New York, seemed restrained, as if trade was desirable as an ill-starred, embarrassing relative.

The hustle of New York's snappy streets made her dizzy. Her sisters would say, "What a donkey you are. Your silly head bounces willy-nilly at everything." She couldn't help herself. Her mouth watered, and her stomach growled from exotic aromas that tugged at her with intangible arms. She almost blurted, "Papa, oh please, can we have a sweet cake with honey and nuts?" She liked the excitement so much she wished they could live in the city, and for an instant forgave Papa for casting her off.

Women in flashy clothing showed naked ankles and peach-colored arms and sniffed at the homely group. Lizzie was astonished by the amount of flesh revealed in airy, soft gowns and the pointy-toed shoes with three-inch heels, disastrous for field work she noted. The smelly contraptions called automobiles emitted terrible bleats when someone stepped in front of them, sounding like a goat crying for its mama, and made her laugh.

When they arrived at the train depot, Adam muscled their two large crates into a freight car, and they boarded the strange contraption that would take them away from the city. The children, behind Adam's back, ran up and down the steel steps until he glared and they slunk off to their seat. Johanna clucked at Lizzie not to lose the four youngsters who stared bug-eyed at the ongoing carnival of sights and sounds from the window of their coach. They could not sit quietly. In the next sentence, Johanna went on to gripe about the greasy sausages and the dry bread loaves bought from sidewalk vendors. "Everyone is gonna get sick. Then what do we do?" Johanna repeated, "What do we do? Lizzie, mind they don't leave their coats," the coats which doubled as blankets.

Lizzie was giddy from all the stimulation. When the train pulled away from the depot, the monumental buildings gradually grew smaller, disappearing miniature towers. They were replaced by the remnants of city life, frail people staring at them from makeshift shacks along the tracks. Her spirits ebbed as the tracks carried them to open fields and onto a monotonous landscape. Johanna jabbered on and on, agitating about a spot of blood on a daughter's jacket, and insisting that Lizzie get water and a cloth to wash it out. After it was cleaned, Johanna pronounced the spot could not be washed away. The sun fell away ahead, and Lizzie hoped that darkness would muffle her. "Go to sleep," Adam grunted. *Go to sleep, Johanna,* Lizzie quietly concurred to the window of the train. *Give us some peace,* she added, whispering to the darkness.

The children's excitement was defeated by the train's clacking wheels and repeated rocking. The intervals grew longer between their declarations of, "Look at that." Finally, their enthusiasm faded to quiet chatter under their jackets. A blond head sprouted then settled against a dark one. Shoulder to shoulder, they slumped down into the wooden seat, a pile of bodies and coats, snuggling little birds in their traveling nest. Lizzie retreated into solitude in the dusky evening as Johanna's demands ceased. Until now the commotion had kept emptiness at bay. In the dark, it returned, the insatiable longing mixed with squelched rage.

When they reached Eureka, South Dakota, they were relieved their travels were behind them, for now they would have a home and land to farm. It was a small town, unlike Hamburg or New York City, but going about its business with the importance and urgency of a major metropolis. They found a spirited rural market scene on the Plains not unlike their home village on another vast prairie. Wagons filled so full of wheat, they looked like they would explode onto the dirt streets, rumbled past them to the railway. They were relieved to hear men shouting greetings in German, the familiar tongue of their colony.

They were a bashful cluster of sheep crowding together on the train platform until a cousin who had previously immigrated from their colony appeared at Adam's side to meet them. Lizzie didn't remember him. He had emigrated when she was eight, but she decided immediately she liked the confident way he took charge. He smiled at her when he helped her lift bundles and he was handsome, with a full head of dark curly hair. He was the color of Adam, but did not share his dour demeanor. He observed Lizzie's awkward movements that hurried to coordinate with her gangly, developing form, admiring her. However, Johanna's many commands to her, clicking in the prairie air like a dissonant chorus of grasshoppers, prevented Lizzie from noticing her cousin's appreciation.

Adam took over an abandoned homestead in Emmons County, North Dakota, and each morning before daylight flooded the prairie, he dictated chores with snorts and glares. The growing family was accustomed to his harshness, but not privy to his consuming fear of failing. Uncertainty gnawed at him constantly about where they could turn to if they did not make it on a farm that had outwitted another homesteader. At dawn the small girls fed the chickens and gathered eggs. Lizzie worked beside Adam to break up sod for planting, and then he rented her out to run a team of horses to disc furrow other farmers' fields. She had no tears left when she fell into the bed she shared with the four small girls. Her back hurt, and her hands were a riot of red sores, seeping blisters that would harden into calluses. As days turned into weeks and weeks into months, she grew muscular and tanned and could lift almost as much as Adam. She disapproved of his ways, but suspected that he believed fear and anger generated more work output. She did what he wanted of her, there was no one to rally for her, but saw in him the same need as his children had, yearning to climb into a mother's protective lap. If she had known her mother, that is what she would have done.

The prairie was perplexing without close neighbors and the communal life they enjoyed in the old country, and Johanna grew unpredictable and less reliable in attending to crucial chores. Coming in from the fields at day's end, Lizzie often would find that supper had not been prepared, yet Johanna insisted that she had made it, and that a robber had stolen it. Lizzie wanted to scream at her, "Just do your part, Johanna. Get ahold of yourself." She resented Johanna for being weak but felt sorry that the woman was perpetually big with child. Johanna cowered when Adam approached or spoke directly to her. Lizzie started making suppers in the morning before she went to the fields then trained the two older girls to take over the kitchen chores.

She recalled the curve in Papa's back that made him seem fragile, and wondered whether it was bending over more these days, and if her sisters were making his supper. They would not be taking good enough care of him. He needed to have a soft boiled egg every morning before he went to the fields. She wanted to complain to him about her circumstances but that was useless, for they had few letters. Lizzie wrote to him once a week, on Sundays when Adam gave in to Johanna's single demand to do no work on the Sabbath. Lizzie hummed his folk tunes when she worked in the fields, the songs Papa had played for her on his accordion before she fell asleep, but she didn't cry anymore in these private minutes.

Adam collected Lizzie from another farm where she had been doing the cooking because Johanna was ponderous with another pregnancy, and needed Lizzie to care for her and the children. "I have too many girls," he chastised Johanna. "I don't want another one," he spoke to the crown of her head. In the two years since they had arrived, Johanna bore two boys, but they would not be helpers for a few years. "The next one better be a boy," he said loudly because he could not tell if she had heard him.

The North Dakota acreage was not fruitful despite their laborious efforts. When Adam heard from his cousin that the Homestead Act had expanded parcel sizes to 320 acres, up from 160, he packed up the family of six children, and another on the way, to move to a claim near Lewistown, Montana. Lizzie had turned sixteen and Adam hired her out to disc, then in the late summer to cook during harvesting on neighboring farms. The older girls worked in the fields with Adam, and he only needed hired help to put in a well.

More than a year later, a fellow German Russian colonist living in the vicinity suggested to Adam that he talk to the banker, Mr. Johnson, in Lewistown who was looking for a maid. The man knew Lizzie's work because she had nursed his wife through a horrible illness and tended to their children. He was impressed with her positive attitude, her smile and tenderness toward his wife despite the unpleasant and difficult chores. He hoped for Lizzie's sake, she could be situated in an environment where she would be well-treated for she had been kind and attentive to his family. She would thrive caring for the banker's house and his five young children he believed. He sweetened the idea for Adam, saying, "I believe they will pay good wages."

Adam calculated. If Lizzie got that job, and they paid good wages, he could use the money, along with the profit from the sale of his wheat and flax, to buy a few head of cattle near Great Falls. He heard the US Army always was in need of more beef. He had sold the first homestead in North Dakota and he believed, if he was careful with every cent he made, he would do better than most and not just squeeze by from one year to the next. He wanted to rest at night and not have to pull the blanket over his head from the fear that poverty would find him.

"Pack your things," Adam ordered Lizzie while she was

cutting doughy *Knepfle* triangles into potato-onion soup one evening. Oh she dreaded those words. He was going to farm her out to someone again.

"Where am I going this time?" How many children would she squeeze among to share a bed, and at whose crowded table would she eat? He shrugged and walked out the door. Johanna was sitting next to the stove, reworking a worn heel on a sock.

"Do you know where I am going?" Lizzie asked. Johanna's lips were pursed as usual, working the darning needle through the sparse threads. Why couldn't Johanna be there for her, to defend her, stand up for her against Adam? Why must *she* always be the strong one?

The cart squeaked toward town the following morning, at various times getting mired in ruts. The wheels were pestles, grinding against clay dirt, soggy from fall weather and frequent vehicles. Adam stopped on Main Street outside a welcoming three-story house. "The banker's place. Mr. Johnson. Hiring for a maid. You get that job!" he pointed at her. She hadn't learned English and Adam didn't explain what she would be expected to do, but she didn't ask and risk him barking in the street about her being stupid.

She nearly tripped off the cart as she absorbed all the details clamoring for her attention. She hadn't felt like this since they were in New York City. She felt tiny, like a doll staring up to the top of the grand house. If the ground-floor windows spoke in honesty, she would be received by kind people.

"Don't act like a dumb potato." She couldn't help it. She was rooted at the yard's edge. Adam pulled her by the elbow up the front steps and onto the porch. He tugged a chord on the side of the glass door that connected to a bell on the inside. It tinkled a fairy sound, and she was pleased with her brother for having mastered the secrets of the New World. A shadow on the opposite side of the prism glass astonished Lizzie with its contorted flashes of red and green bouncing about and owned by whoever would open the door. It seemed magical, and she laughed.

Adam scowled.

That crazy quilt of red and green pieces turned out to be an elegant woman wholly in one piece upon opening the door. "Oh," Lizzie gushed in her German dialect, "I will get this job," and almost clapped her hands.

The woman smiled. "Hello, you must be Lizzie"—reaching out for her hand—"and I am Mrs. Johnson." Lizzie would work for nothing if they didn't like her well enough to pay her! Mrs. Johnson led them through the foyer and into the parlor, where Lizzie saw enormous velvet chairs stuffed like plump ducks in teal-green and russet tones. The windows were so tall God could peer inside and not be disappointed. Then she pictured Johanna sitting at the crude table in the large room of their shack, where the morning sunlight was struggling to get through the one small window on the east side.

Mrs. Johnson talked rapidly, and Lizzie looked from her to Adam trying to catch the idea of what they were saying. At times, Mrs. Johnson spoke directly to her, smiling and nodding her head up and down vigorously, as though this would clarify what she said. In German, Adam repeated the duties. "You got the job. Work hard and keep your nose to yourself. No sniffling about Papa."

Adam and Mrs. Johnson made arrangements about Lizzie's wages, agreeing that he would come at the end of each month to collect them. He gave a proper European bow to Mrs. Johnson, then without a glance toward Lizzie, vanished from the parlor and melted out of sight as the wagon pulled away.

Two youngsters, the smallest of the Johnson children, watched Lizzie through the lower posts of the banister and hid their faces behind chubby hands when Lizzie said to Mrs. Johnson in German, "I don't speak no English." She was ashamed as though it was her fault.

They thought they could not be seen, but Lizzie turned around to find them. When she discovered them behind the bars, two friendly faced animals peering from their cage, she laughed. "Hallo," she whispered loudly. The three older siblings, on the landing above, stared over the railing and frowned at her severe-looking clothing, while their mother continued to talk in a gentle voice.

When Mrs. Johnson led her upstairs to her room, she got dizzy looking over the banister. The buildings in Hamburg and New York City had forced her to search for the sky between their roofs. Now she was looking below her and must adjust to living so far removed from solid ground!

Mrs. Johnson gestured toward the dresser and opened the top drawer, pointing to Lizzie's hemp sack. "This is your room now, Lizzie." After Mrs. Johnson left the room, Lizzie hugged herself, falling back onto the bed and laughing. "I have my own room, Papa!"

In Papa's house there was a main floor and the attic which the children shared. The space was sufficient for the large family because of the age differences. The older ones married young and moved out, but no bed remained empty very long as more children were born.

In North Dakota, Lizzie had visited the home of her cousin's friend, another German Russian colonist, who lived and worked in town. He had a three-story house, the first home she was inside of with more than one floor. It was grand. *Maybe I will have a house like this someday,* she mused.

As he vowed, Adam came the last day of each month to collect her wages. Lizzie did not see him for several months because either she was with the children when he came or helping Mrs. Johnson with errands. He didn't ask after her. He dropped the few silver dollars into his leather pouch and evaporated.

Lizzie began working for the Johnsons in October, and it was on the last day of March before she saw her brother again. It would be a day she would never forget. It was her eighteenth birthday and she was flushed and giddy with the preparations in the kitchen, for Mrs. Johnson and the children and she were in the process of baking cookies.

"Come on, Lizzie," the children urged. "Guess what your presents are."

She laughed. "Oh, I don't care. I am already so happy!" Four years earlier, before being packed off from Russia, she had celebrated her fourteenth birthday with Papa. That recollection folded itself into the festivities with the good-hearted Johnsons.

Papa had returned from the fields to find Lizzie's elder sister, Maria, making thin pancakes from a runny batter that she spread with berry preserves and rolled into cylinders. "What's this, then?" Papa asked, pretending not to know the reason for this special dish. "Oh, Papa." Lizzie's hurt face tugged at him, and he pulled her to his lap where he produced a gold music box with a dancing ballerina on top.

A few days later he announced in a firm voice, "You will go with Adam to America." She cried until her chest ached and gripped tight. Maria chided, "Look at that beet nose. I guess we can add it to our borscht!" Lizzie was sure Papa would change his mind when he saw she was not letting go of her misery. But her tears did not move him. In his own bed, he wept as copiously as she, and for many days his eyes were red and swollen.

She protected the gift on every part of the journey to her new home. On the sea voyage, she stored the music box treasure in a small basket and cushioned it on the train from New York. Each time they moved she wrapped it in thick rags and cradled it as if it were Johanna's latest baby. In rare moments, when she was able to move without knocking other elbows, she listened to its tinkling melody. But Lizzie kept it away from the children who lurched around the small kitchen, swinging their siblings as if they were outdoors, throwing pots and pans, while Johanna ignored the bedlam, seldom returning from her solitary place.

Lizzie's favorite place to whisper her complaints to Papa about Adam, or how Johanna watched and criticized, was a clutch of birch and cottonwoods at the corner of Adam's acreage. "I work very hard to do things like they want," she assured Papa. "Adam doesn't like me. He's mean. You should have listened to me," she scolded, "but, if you let me come back, I'll make you very happy. I'll make your eggs just as you like them," she smiled. Her invisible Papa sat with her, paring an apple and handing her pieces as he sliced them with his ancient pocketknife. He talked to her about the weather in the language of farmers. "We sure need the rain." It didn't matter what Papa talked about. She just wanted to hear the rumble of his low voice and let it spread over her like a goose-down comforter.

The Johnson kitchen cheered when the front door bell tinkled. Lizzie rushed to answer expecting Horace Whitney, the young teller from the bank who often delivered messages to Mrs. Johnson, and who was coming to the birthday party. It was the last day of the month, but Adam's appearance, regular as the Sunday church bell, had been forgotten.

At the bank, Mr. Johnson's office was situated with a view of his employee, and frequently he boomed through the open door, "Horace, go tell Mrs. Johnson to set another place for dinner." Lydia Johnson would chuckle when she came to the front door. "Thank you for warning me, Horace." There was no point asking who would be coming, for it was likely Horace was not informed.

"Lizzie, set another plate for dinner," she repeated in the kitchen. But some days, Mrs. Johnson took pity on the fellow, whose talents were wasted on errands and the tedious adding and subtracting of numbers and queried, "Have you had any home-baked cookies with coffee today, Horace?" although she knew Mr. Johnson would expect Horace to return promptly to the bank. If Mr. Johnson later complained, "You are hog-tying my employee, Lydia," she flirted. "A fifteen-minute break isn't going to hurt either the bank or Horace, dear."

There were many afternoons when Mrs. Johnson and Lizzie made pastries and the kitchen came alive in their culinary playground. The counters and the floor brimmed with flour, salt, eggs, and cream, and bowls and wooden spoons. They had such gay times together. Lizzie often desired to put her arms around the older woman and tell her, "I wish you were my mother." The older children were at school, the younger ones on the floor banging on pots and pans and enchanting Mrs. Johnson with their "kitchen music." Little hands molded dough until it turned gray and then was put in pans for the oven. Among that cacophony of scents and noise, Horace saw Lizzie for the first time. Her sleeves were rolled up to her elbows, and she was lifting her head from a child who had planted a kiss on her nose leaving a dusting of flour on it. He laughed out loud, and she smiled back and said, "Hello." Every day since, Horace hoped Mr. Johnson would ask him to take a message to his wife.

Before they had children, Lydia walked to the bank each noon, carrying a tray with hot soup and warm biscuits. Mr. Johnson fussed. He was tormented between satisfying his wife and maintaining decorum. She said brightly, "Dear, we have enough decorum. Let's squander some of it," and squeezed his arm.

Even the times he thought he won an argument he was uneasy, for he suspected he had lost something. He was comfortable at the bank where he could tally the day's deposits and withdrawals and make figures agree. The exchanges with his wife made him anxious at times, as though he was overlooking something that, at the end of the day, would result in an imbalance. After the arrival of the first child, she came to the bank with cold meat sandwiches. In the beginning, he hardly noticed, but as this became the normal fare, he longed for her robust soups. By the time the second child settled in, she packed him an apple and a chicken leg from a previous dinner. When the third child came, lunches were no longer mentioned.

His wife was a detective for uncovering new romance for she spotted flirtations before the people involved recognized their own ardor. It didn't require much investigating, however, when Horace was taken captive in the kitchen. Mrs. Johnson kept a stash of amorous novels by her bedside to entertain her on the evenings Mr. Johnson was "thinking about your bank." She'd like to be a matchmaker, but Horace didn't need any help from her.

Nevertheless, Mrs. Johnson did her best to cultivate the blossom. She invited Horace to popcorn-popping evenings when Mr. Johnson attended board meetings. Mr. Johnson was pragmatic. He weighed with great caution the loans he granted or denied, and he required that Horace, his sole bank employee, be vigilant with the bank's assets, and that his personal behavior be beyond reproach. But, as might be predicted, Lydia Johnson refused to conform to Mr. Johnson's tallied standard. This was confounding yet exhilarating for him.

"Hello, dear," she hurried to greet him when the front door closed behind him. He was overrun and defeated before he hung up his hat and coat in the foyer. After a measured day of dollars and punctilious clients, he was not prepared for a whimsical atmosphere, but Lydia's wet kiss—right on the lips, for goodness' sake—and the tug into her warm bosom, separated him from his reluctance.

Lizzie skipped down the hallway from the kitchen, trailing a handful of multicolored ribbons for decorating. When she reached the door and threw it open, she exclaimed, "Horace, come look what we're making!" Adam stared back.

It took a moment to regain her footing. "Adam," she whispered and then went numb. For six wonderful months she had not had to endure his scrutiny and criticism, his moods, or being hired out. He, and Johanna, and the children were as distant and foreign as Papa had become. Sometimes she had a random memory, but she did not miss them or want to see them, and she was certain that as long as she was making money for Adam, she would be free of his temper and his dictates. But, the sudden tightness in her throat, and the sweaty palms, told her in that moment that everything she had come to love was going to be taken away, and she panicked. She turned away from Adam, but something stopped her from running.

If she was stunned, Adam was unnerved. In all the previous months, Mrs. Johnson had received him and she paid the wages. Instead, he was greeted by a sister whose head was uncovered. She'd opened the door with a wide-open smile that had frozen, and not yet slipped away. The volume of hair shocked him, the tiny, insolent wisps flowering about her forehead. He took a step back.

"Adam," her voice dropped an octave. She floundered trying to recall how to act toward her brother. Although Lizzie was the maid, Mrs. Johnson and she shared the duties of answering the door to callers. Mrs. Johnson sniffed, turned up her nose at the thought of having servants. "You're here to help me, not be my slave," she cautioned Lizzie.

When Lizzie answered the door, she greeted callers with "Good afternoon" and "Won't you come in?" leading guests, her shoulders straight and tall, into the fancy parlor with parquet flooring and tall windows adorned with buttery brocade drapes. But this was her brother, and he stood in the doorway wearing his drab garments as if they had been carried in the womb with him and were born his twin. Lizzie's hearty confidence sunk along with her festive smile.

His muscular shoulders swelled his bleak coat. She talked in English. She hadn't spoken German these many months. Her liveliness lingered briefly, not wanting to be let go for it would not come again. Then, it floated like a kite caught up on a gentle pocket of wind.

Spirits in the kitchen were soaring as the children anticipated seeing Horace, but instead, a cold draft drifted in. They looked to their mother, "Oh," Mrs. Johnson gasped, remembering, "The end of the month," and hurried to the foyer just in time to hear Adam say in German, "You're leaving, NOW!" Mrs. Johnson might not understand his words, but she got the gist when Lizzie brushed past her and up the stairs.

"Lizzie," Mrs. Johnson cried reaching out but missing her sleeve. She turned. "Adam is something wrong?"

"I come to take Lizzie home," he said, eyeing a floor tile.

"But I don't understand," Mrs. Johnson said.

"Lizzie's needed back home, Missus. I come for her and her last wages."

He stood in the foyer, broad as an ancient oak, while the flustered Mrs. Johnson retrieved the money from her husband's study. The children followed Lizzie up to her room, crowding around her. "How are we going to have your party if you're not here, Lizzie?" She solved every one of their many tangled problems and tears but could not fix this one.

The wagon drove off on the road that was muddy now from the spring rains. The showers would promise a good harvest. Somber faces watched through the parlor windows. Mrs. Johnson produced a tentative wave from the magnificent porch where Lizzie and Horace had talked on warm evenings. The banker's wife clutched the edge of her apron in despair. For the moment she could not be like the women she touted who fought against rules meant to keep them in their place, women in charge of their own decisions. In Montana, women farmed their own land. Some came to Mr. Johnson's bank and applied for loans or started savings accounts. Even Mr. Johnson, with fixed views of a woman's place, was impelled to adjust for these customers, some of whom proved to be financial wizards.

As the cart was pulling away Horace was only just arriving at the Johnson house. Mr. Johnson had handed him unexpected paper work which had delayed him. He was in misery watching the clock hand lurch forward and subtracting the time he could be with Lizzie. He did not consider the girl on the wooden bench with head scarf and dark clothing as it passed by. The Lizzie who had teased and laughed with him and wore pretty pastel dresses, did not look back at him.

Because Mrs. Johnson blurred the lines between employer and employee to match her progressive views, she and Lizzie had formed a close relationship. They were alike in some ways. Although Mrs. Johnson came from some wealth and education, she and Lizzie concurred that, no matter the race or gender, everyone should have equal rights. This thinking was revolutionary for Lizzie, and fostered and encouraged by Mrs. Johnson.

Mr. Johnson, however, subscribed to a natural hierarchy, so Lizzie baffled him. He could not quite acquiesce, but reluctantly agreed the girl had an uncanny wit paired with practical intelligence. His children were privileged by circumstances and unschooled in hardships, and yet Lizzie taught them how to manage with few assets. She made a game of it and they loved her for it, and were proud of what they learned. She showed how to reuse torn clothing and repair a broken shoe, and what to do with sour milk. His children were cordial toward visitors, and even when guests were not present, they exhibited polite table manners. He expected proper behavior from them and assumed he was the credit for their success, but he was puzzled at their alacrity when Lizzie wanted a particular result, and they were ready to meet it.

"Lizzie, where are you going?" Horace gasped when he recognized it was Lizzie who had passed him in the cart. He ran down the street shouting after her. She either could not, or refused to hear him above the noise from the wagon's wheels squawking and squealing, and the hooves pounding like hammers against half-frozen ground. She was looking down at her folded hands, while Adam sat rigid, scowled at his horse, and rattled the reins to speed the animal along.

Mrs. Johnson trembled, waving a white hanky with rosebuds Lizzie had embroidered along its edges. She cleared her throat to stop the tears. "Oh my Lord. Oh my Lord," she repeated, watching the butt of the wagon jiggling down the street. "She's eighteen today," she announced to no one, for she was alone on the porch. "She hasn't opened her presents, yet," picturing the lavender dress the children had picked out and wrapped. How could she and the children—and Horace— bear the rest of this day? She ached to go in the house and upstairs to sleep, for she could not fix it with the children, or Horace, and especially herself. She dreaded going in there and putting aside her feelings to listen to the children, who would not stop asking her, "Why?" She didn't know why. She had stood up to Mr. Johnson about women getting the vote. She told him she would see that happen, and that goal seemed far easier than getting Lizzie returned by her bullheaded brother.

"Mrs. Johnson. What's going on? That was Lizzie in that cart!" Horace raced up the steps. She nodded. "Come inside, Horace."

Lizzie refused to dwell on what she left behind. She did not permit the memories to stick around when they floated up. She pushed them down angrily, and vowed she would not end up like Johanna who had not come to terms with her circumstances. The only way she would stay strong was to forget, and to stop caring. She had blunted the horror of being ripped away from Papa. She had learned how to stop her feelings. She would do it again.

She'd been naïve believing she was safe and could laugh and love again, and be loved by the Johnsons'. She had even shared her history with Mrs. Johnson while mashing potatoes and cutting up vegetables. Mrs. Johnson had been as compassionate as someone can be without knowing what it was like to be ripped away from someone you loved. Mrs. Johnson had been tender, but Lizzie would not get attached again. No good could come from it, only sorrow.

Even Mrs. Johnson, with all her talk of freedom and the vote for women, in the end, stood helpless on the empty porch, unable to soften the sting. Lizzie buried the sting. She tucked it away before the wagon got out of town, shut it up in a compartment to keep it prisoner, and allowed it neither light nor nourishment. Otherwise, she could not do even the simple things like dressing and feeding herself.

She had not fought against leaving for her brother's face had shocked her. She felt like she'd been hit in the face with icy well water. Adam was a man hurrying into old age, chased by relentless work and worry. She obeyed his order to return to the shack and Johanna, and made no objection, while the Johnson family stood by and watched, confounded and aggrieved.

Johanna lumbered under the weight of her ninth pregnancy. The small of her back was a fist pummeling at her, but she felt relief when tongue-lashing Lizzie. She blamed either Adam or Lizzie, often not able to distinguish between the two, for the frequency and discomfort of her pregnancies. Johanna was loyal to the old country ways but could not find the shovel big enough to dig herself out of the longing and depression that shared space with each of the babies as they waited to be born. Adam spoke sharply to her, and over time her nerves stayed taut, and her mind grew rigid.

Their nearest neighbor, Mrs. Andersson, encouraged a friendship. Every week the neighboring women congregated at her friend Mirna's place where they softened the pockets of winter loneliness. Mrs. Andersson encouraged Johanna to come into their circle, but the language barrier, and her adherence to her ways, left her even more isolated. During one gathering, Bertha, a woman who had German grandparents and remembered bits of the language, attempted a conversation to no avail. Even Mirna, who maintained her silent boundary at her loom during their social afternoons, brought Johanna a cup of coffee. Yet Johanna did not make a connection with any of them.

Johanna was religiously devoted to the home ways of the German Russian colony, and they guided how she functioned in the austere environment. She wanted her children to imitate and carry on her beliefs. During the winters, when Adam could not use them, they entered school. There they mixed with others their own ages and learned English. Their mama's ways embarrassed them.

Lizzie could not escape to school like the children. The day he brought her back, Adam slammed the door of the shack and holed up in the barn. Johanna, swaddled in baby fat, slipped into a fleeting clear moment brought on by Lizzie's return and her husband's outburst. She snickered. Consciousness flickered briefly then tumbled into a jumble, crashing as it had ascended. As confusion took control again, Johanna wept. Between sobs she screamed, "You owe us! You owe us for the rest of your life!"

Lizzie was resting under the golden cottonwoods when Horace rode onto the homestead. She didn't have a view of the shack, but if she had, she would have been relieved that she was not there to receive him. Adam would chase him off, but because she did not know this, she did not have to bear the shame. She cranked up the music box. She seldom listened to it for she was no longer a fourteen year old girl who lived with Papa. He would not approve of what she believed due to the influence of living with the Johnsons. She worked hard, and that would still please him, and she didn't want to disappoint him, but he would not accept women choosing their own course, or speaking up, or fighting to change laws.

"You're like Mr. Johnson, I think," she told Papa, remembering the stoical man who brightened only when his wife was nearby.

"Oh Papa, Adam is so old, and no nicer. He growls worse than before because he has that herd of cattle now. And you should see, Johanna. Someone has to watch out for her. That's why I came back, Papa. Oh, I wanted to stay with the

Johnsons. I couldn't bear to look back when we drove away. Just like when I left you. Do you remember, Papa?" She rewound the music box. "I know you don't want to hear this, but I want to be like those women Mrs. Johnson talks about." Before she learned that a woman could make her decisions on her own, she had not questioned how Adam worked her. All the women worked for their man and followed his orders. That was the ways of things, and that's why she never complained. She imagined Papa being proud and telling her, "You're a good girl, Lizzie." But being a good girl meant she must stay with Adam and work hard without complaint. A part of her still wanted to please Papa, and in one ear she heard the words "loyalty" and "obedience." In the other, the suffragettes preached independence, and in their prison cells refused to eat, not allowing the law to force them into submission because of their beliefs, and thus had feeding tubes stuffed down their throats.

Johanna's children were attending school and Adam was on a trip to Great Falls when Mrs. Johnson came. Although the cottonwoods had shed the bulk of their leaves, the days were still mild, and Lizzie was spreading laundry over a line in the warm rays. She saw a sole woman on a horse but did not recognize her former employer. Johanna, inside nursing the most recent baby, heard the talking near the shack. The wretched hand of fate granted her the misfortune of a sane moment just then. From the crude window her fragile universe collided with the reality, exposing her like her nursing breast. She choked back a scream, the kind that infuriated Adam. The same kind she yelled during her dreams when she walked naked through their Russian village with no place to hide.

Mrs. Johnson's clothing was rich gold and black, her hair coiled in a fashionable twist under a small velvet hat with an exaggerated emerald-green feather. The breeze snapped at the laundry, and crisp shirt sleeves and apron strings sparred with the feather. Johanna watched them laughing, although she did not regard Lizzie's hesitation as Mrs. Johnson did.

Johanna put her hands over her ears to keep out their foreign words. Trapped in a sticky web that held her near the window she threw her ankle-length apron over her face. Their voices were the voices of the spirits that whispered inside the walls in the dead of night. A far-off call commanded she put down the long-bladed knife she had grabbed from the table. After Mrs. Johnson rode off, Lizzie did not mention the visitor, and Johanna could not distinguish between the visitor and the nocturnal frequenters tarrying, like a layer of dust, on the dresser.

Lizzie continued working under Adam's exacting eye. Johanna stopped producing children and grew edgier, her reasoning pushed off-balance by some invisible force. She forgot the names and faces of her children, because too many bodies that looked alike occupied the same space over the prolonged winter. Any loud noise agitated her and caused her to roll her head in circles, first clockwise, then the reverse, till her eyes swam frantically from one corner to the other like fish in a bowl looking for an exit. At night she cried out, saying she would tattle to Papa or her brother, Christian, who had remained behind in Russia, to get out the hickory stick. Adam growled and left to sleep with his animals in the barn. He blamed her, thought she was goading him for taking her away from her family. He brushed off her outbursts and continued to build up his livestock, attending to them rather than his children or wife.

Winter was coming that first year when Lizzie encountered Horace in her stand of cottonwoods. It had been eight months since he ran after her cart the day she left with Adam, and she ignored him. He was uneasy, not the jovial young man she remembered who had teased her.

From what Mrs. Johnson had reported when she visited the homestead, Horace did not laugh very much, and he had stopped coming to their popcorn evenings. "None of us— and that includes Mr. Johnson—are the same since you left. It would make us all so happy if you came back."

"I can't come back." She motioned toward the shack. She saw Johanna's profile in the window.

"But certainly *sometime* you can, Lizzie. It must be very hard for you here. I can see by your hands how hard you're working." She rested her hand on Lizzie's sleeve. "You aren't in the old country anymore. Your papa isn't here to decide how you should live. You know about the women who are fighting against just that." The women in Montana were going to get the vote, and it wasn't because they had been dutiful and waited for a generous man to grant this right. Lizzie could earn a living on her own. She had done so each time Adam sent her out to work. Mrs. Johnson told her that obligation could be honorable only if fair to all parties; otherwise, it was a weapon used to imprison. Lizzie's jaw was firm. Mrs. Johnson's strong words could not convince her.

Some of the old beliefs lived within Lizzie still. Mrs. Johnson could see there was more to her resistance than just Adam's demands. Lizzie dreaded her choleric brother, whose silence felt menacing and froze any chance for a civil word between them. He couldn't rest if a field was left unfinished or his animals were not fed on time. But she understood that behind his demeanor there was the horror of having to shoulder everything. Johanna could not be his helpmate, and there was no one else.

"Horace came to see you," Mrs. Johnson said. "Did you know that?"

"When?" Lizzie shivered and pictured him being sent off their land. The grass had turned brown from the summer heat. She imagined him riding over it and up to the shack to extend his hand, expecting it would be reciprocated.

"Weeks ago. Your brother didn't tell you?"

Lizzie studied the sheets sailing with the wind. "No, of course not," Mrs. Johnson answered her own question.

"Horace said that he will come again and again until he sees you. But Lizzie, I told him that might cause you more harm than good. We talked it over with Mr. Johnson and decided it best if I came, and Mr. Johnson said he will come if all else fails, because Adam has been to see him about a loan."

It was on a Sunday that Lizzie saw Horace under her batch of trees. For Johanna, the Sabbath day was important if she was cognizant of what day it was. Adam mostly ignored Johanna insistence that only necessary chores be handled and spent the day with his cattle.

"If Horace wants to see me," Lizzie had told Mrs. Johnson, "he can find me in the copse on a Sunday afternoon."

The branches of the white birch were barren and were a keen contrast against the inky-gray sky. A biting north wind forewarned an arctic snap, promising a snowstorm. The brooding clouds signaled a sharp temperature drop, and Horace had bundled up in his woolens. He arrived first and wondered if Lizzie would come. He was shivering, and he clapped his hands inside their mittens, and stamped his boots against a rotting birch log. He was sure she was not going to come then caught sight of a dark-clad figure bucking the wind to get headway. The tail end of her head scarf swung about like an appendage. She held her arms crossed in an X to keep the edges of her coat together.

She was huffing but smiled shyly when she approached the trees. The pair settled on her favorite log, but the wind gave bear roars, and they cupped their hands to each other's ears to talk. When they grew frustrated with the yelling, they shrugged and laughed, for it was hopeless, and held hands. He grasped the end of her scarf when it slapped them in their faces, but the squall gale was insistent, tugging at the scarf to torment it. He corralled the cloth with his arm over her shoulder, glad to have a reason to hold her close. But the storm was dogged and forced them to end their meeting, despite trying to resist its insistence. Wet snow began to fall, and the wind got even angrier, and Lizzie signaled they must leave. Horace would ram into the wind going back to town; Lizzie would get swatted from behind going home.

One year after leaving the Johnsons, Horace met her again among the birches. He paced like a penned-up wolf waiting for her. Cocoon-shaped blossoms dangled from the branches, some plopping down to make a generous golden bed at the feet of the trunks. He caught sight of her running toward him, her scarf fluttering behind delighted him, and he raced to meet her. He was sorry her lovely hair was covered and could not fly behind her to catch the spring light.

She tapped him on the sleeve as she caught her breath. "I thought you might be here today." He felt happy again. They rested on her log where they'd shivered in the fall, and Horace took her hand that had the callused edges, and the fingernails untended. Premature lines teased about her eyes and forehead.

"I can't stay long." He waited for her to say more, but when she didn't, he said, "I have something important to tell you, but first we must share a picnic basket." She smiled then looked over her left shoulder.

"Mrs. Johnson and the children made sandwiches, your favorite egg salad, and they baked the butter cookies with pink frosting you love."

"Adam was saddling his horse before I left. He's out checking fences and will come this way." He wondered if she heard him.

"You have to eat something, Lizzie. I can't go back and tell them you didn't try it all," he insisted, handing her a sandwich with a bright-red ribbon the children prepared for her.

"Oh, they told me to warn you not to bite down hard. I

almost forgot," he laughed. "There's a surprise in it." She nibbled a corner, then took a small bite and felt something metallic. She poked it with her tongue then followed the curved edge until she came to a hard piece, which she grabbed between her lips. She sucked pieces of egg off until the stone shone like the blue cornflower.

"It's a yogo sapphire from over in the Little Belts." He was glowing a bit.

"Look at that color," she cried, forgetting to look over her shoulder. "It is so clear and bright!"

"Like a mountain stream," he agreed.

"But, you must take it back to them," she announced at once and held it out to him. "I can't keep this."

He nearly fell off the log. "But, Lizzie, it isn't from them. It's from me." He laughed and told her that he had wanted to give it to her for months. "It was the foul weather that made me wait this long," he grimaced.

"The bank is sending me to Helena to become the manager. Can you believe that? Mr. Johnson told them I am up to the job! So, the only thing left is for me to marry you and take you with me. If you will have me, Lizzie." His pleading face seemed pathetic but she resisted the temptation to kiss him.

She felt like a rope being pulled at both ends. "Horace." She said finally. She had the ring tucked against her heart as if to protect it. Horace sucked in his breath. Her eyes were closed, and he waited for her to open them, he studied her, adoring the cute curve of her slanted eyes. He tried to second guess her, he was determined to read what he wanted to hear her say, but when she opened them again, she said flatly, "You must take it back, Horace. I can't go with you."

He sucked his breath in again, and waited a second. *Give her a minute*, he told himself. *She didn't expect this. Don't rush her.* He'd been too hasty.

"I don't mean right now, Lizzie. I know you've got to settle things here. I'll come back for you next Sunday." He was ash gray, and his fingers shook. He could not comprehend that she would say no despite Mrs. Johnson having cautioned him that it might not be easy. How *could* she stay with an abusive brother when he was offering her a way out?

"No, Horace. I can't go with you—now or next Sunday." She wished she could tell him how much she wanted to be with him. But that would encourage him and the result would come out the same. A horse and rider were in the distance along the fence line, headed away from them. Adam was leaning over his horse searching for breaks, but if he didn't find broken wire, he would be turning and heading back soon.

"I have to go now," she said abruptly. Johanna could not be left on her own for long. She had taken to wandering off at strange times, sometimes sneaking out of the shack during the night. Once they found her at the well, trying to climb into the bucket. When the children were at school, Lizzie cared for her. If the children watched her, they often forgot her, which then led to a search party. Johanna walked almost the whole way into Lewistown once before they realized she was missing.

Horace also saw Adam. "Meet me back here next Sunday, please," he implored. "We can talk about it next time."

She studied Adam's thick back and shook her head. "No, Horace. Don't come again. I can't marry you." She bit her lip almost making it bleed to hold back her tears, then put the ring back on his palm.

"Lizzie." He was hoarse. "That ring was meant for you. It couldn't belong to anyone else. I had it made special when I went to Helena."

"I can't keep it," she said fiercely.

"Maybe, if nothing else, it will bring you good luck, and maybe you will remember me and our happy times. And you will think well of me?"

Her eyes were pasted onto the hindquarters of Adam's horse. "I'll never forget you, Horace. They were the best days of my life," she said quietly.

Adam arrived at the corner of his property, just when Lizzie darted out of the copse. Shouting at Horace over her shoulder, she repeated, "The *very* best days, Horace. Thank you. Thank you." He couldn't see the tears streaming, or when she was far enough away not to be heard, that she bellowed like a calf to the sky.

Horace was about to shout after her, but saw that Adam was turning the horse in the direction of the cottonwoods. Adam stopped suddenly, jumped off his horse to check a tilting post, tugging and pushing against it to see if it held firm. Horace felt as empty as Adam's acreage, spread out on the huge table of earth. And, like Adam's barbed wire that snapped and sagged, Horace felt the support holding his perimeter together coming undone.

On Lizzie' twenty-first birthday, Adam charged his oldest daughter to watch over Johanna and Lizzie to go with him to town to help carry sacks of feed. He no longer hired her out because of Johanna, whose health slipped out of her like water in a leaky bucket, and required that Lizzie clean, dress, and feed her.

Lizzie was working the weekly bread dough, and pulled the sticky last bits off her fingers. She covered the mixture with the dish towel to keep it free of drafts. "Knead it when it doubles," she reminded the girl, hoping she would have her wits around her. She pulled the apron over her head, handed it to the girl. "Take your mama to the outhouse, even if she makes a fuss about it." The girl nodded but stared out the opened door, distant and dreamy as her mama.

Birthdays in Adam's house got up in the morning and slipped into the floorboard cracks long before midday. When a calf was born, however, Adam drank a glass of the homemade brew Mrs. Andersson brought on one of her visits to Johanna.

The road was muddy as it had been when she left the Johnsons three years ago. She didn't often get to town, but instead of stopping at the feed store, Adam headed straight for the surveyor's office. "My sister here is taking out her claim," he said, and produced the immigration papers verifying Lizzie's age. So he did know it was her birthday!

Adam and his precious herd—and land. So, that was what he had planned! For her to be twenty-one when he could use her once again to increase his land holdings and build up his livestock.

In Bessarabia when she was a little girl, traveling performers came through their village and set up orange-and-white-striped tents and told stories using painted wooden figures with strings attached to arms, legs, and heads. Adam held her strings. *For now,* she whispered. She felt Papa's eyes on her, watching from the corner of the land office. He held out the music box to her with the ballerina standing on one pointed foot. She could run out of the land office now! Go to Helena, and march in a parade with a sash emblazoned with FREEDOM across it.

"Why *today* is your twenty-first birthday," the young man confirmed, looking through the document. Adam gestured. "She's going to make a claim on the 320 acres next to my homestead." The young man kept his eyes on Lizzie. He smiled. "Happy birthday"—he searched for her name on the paper—"Lizzie." She shrugged but was embarrassed. Adam looked at her, too, and did not approve that the man spoke to her directly, not to him.

"Are you married?" His eyes were still on her. "Because then the claim must be made in your husband's name. Or divorced or widowed?"

"She ain't married. Just her, and twenty-one. Not married," Adam repeated. "Never married." The young man looked at Lizzie waiting for her to affirm this. She nodded quickly keeping her eyes on the desk.

"You have to live on the land, and build a shack," he reminded her. She nodded again. "And, if you *do* get married," he emphasized, "you understand the land will become your husband's property."

"She knows all that. And, she ain't getting mar…."

"When can I meet you, Lizzie, to go over the property and assess it?" he interrupted, cutting Adam's sentence short.

"She already knows the land. We been living next to it for more than five years. Just look at them papers there," Adam pointed to the documents he brought with him.

"That's all well and good," the clerk insisted, "but we'll need to see if we've got apples and not oranges."

"There ain't no apples and no oranges," Adam pressed.

"I'll survey for assets and deficiencies. So," he asked Lizzie again, "when do you want to go over the property?"

"I'll be the one who goes over it," Adam declared.

"No sir," the clerk said, and Lizzie's head flew up. She couldn't help herself for it stunned her so. The young man was used to dealing with all sorts of claimants, some who tried to steal free land. "The claim's in her name. She'll be responsible to meet the requirements, sign the documents, and review the land with me."

"You come to my place to get her, then," Adam told him, demanding the last word.

"My name is John Herbert," he told her, shaking her hand after helping her into his Model T. Johanna's children hung by the door of the shack, ogling, and when the car drove off, they chased after it, eating its dust. "I already know yours." He blushed because she smiled at him. "I know," she said.

It was a brilliant day. Buttercups laced the stubby green grasses, and their shoes got soaked from stepping over and trying to avert the puddles on the property. John Herbert measured exact boundaries. He was careful and precise. Yet, he was friendly and spoke in a manner that put her at ease, despite Adam following behind on his horse. Not since Horace had a man spoken so gently to her. She almost forgot about Adam who was keeping three hundred yards between them the whole time. John Herbert said, "You do know your brother has been following us ever since we left your place." She wouldn't tell this stranger that she knew where Adam was. Always.

"Doesn't he let you see anyone?" She put her hand over her forehead to block the sun.

"He thinks he should be doing this. Not me."

"Why not?" John was the son of an immigrant. He had been raised with the rigid rules carried over from the old country that in America seemed incongruous and inflexible.

"Do you ever go to the dances?" he asked, sounding hopeful.

She shook her head. "Not ever," she whispered. Horace taught her to dance on the porch at the Johnsons. She'd blushed when he guided her arm over his shoulder, and took her other hand in his. She couldn't remember which arm went over the shoulder anymore. Horace was gone off to Helena to a new life and that was the end of her dancing and Horace.

"I could take you sometime. There's one this Saturday. At the schoolhouse. Hank Perkins makes that fiddle sing and he really gets things going."

"I can't."

"You'd like it," he smiled sadly. "I know you would," but wondered if it was because of him or Adam that she turned him down.

Lizzie moved into her make-do shack at the beginning of June. Each evening, she put Johanna to bed and saw to the dishes, then went back to her own place. *Alone.* She started a garden, put in carrots, potatoes, beets, and corn, and Adam brought her two plum trees. She hauled her water from Adam's while managing both households, and tending to Johanna. The older of Johanna's girls avoided their mother, abhorring her vacant stares, her outbursts and slobbering, and they failed to watch out for her. They sassed Lizzie if she reprimanded them, and hid kitchen things to provoke her if Adam was not there. They envied Lizzie's beauty and the calm strength she demonstrated when Johanna was having one of her dreadful fits.

Johanna disappeared one blistering afternoon while Lizzie was hoeing corn and the girls were in charge of attending her. Lizzie was the first to discover her gone when she came in to prepare supper.

"Where is your mama?" she bristled at the eldest, who shrugged her off and made a face. Lizzie ran out to the well. She hadn't crawled in there. She headed to the road and shouted at Adam who was hauling water out to his cattle that were gasping from the heat. It dawned on the girls, however late, that something was wrong, and they darted in and out of rows of cabbages. Creamy streaks of evening light covered the landscape before Adam almost stumbled over his wife partially hidden in a patch of sagebrush a mile away. He carried her limp body back to the shack. She was no heavier than a sack of seed. Lizzie wet her cracked lips with a damp cloth, and then tried to get her to swallow sips of water. She continued to live for three days. At times she awoke and cried out for her papa and her brother. Once, she said it was not her fault the gate was open and the horses got out. On the third day she sat up in bed and said, "I won't go to America with Adam. He can't make me go." She screamed and fell back and died.

In the fall, after the harvest was in, Adam and Lizzie built a barn on her claim. Then, he headed for Great Falls to buy milkers, and sows for her to tend through the winter. With Johanna gone, she found time for herself in the evenings. She discovered she liked to study after she came across a fourth level McGuffey Reader that Johanna's children left neglected. It was a damp fall evening when John Herbert appeared with a box of apples. She had a small fire going in the stove. He smelled the smoke before he got to the shack and saw her through her small window sitting in the candlelight. She heard the footsteps before he knocked, and thought it must be Adam come to fuss at her about one of the milkers that was limping.

John Herbert's big smile vanished as soon as she opened the door and, instead of greeting him and appreciating the lovely fruit, she looked perplexed. He'd hoped she would be pleased to see him again.

"You really shouldn't be here," she said hoarsely. "My brother wouldn't like it."

"I won't stay," he promised. "I brought you some apples, see?"

She glanced at them, and then looked over his shoulder into the dusky night. He turned to see what she was looking at but there was nothing to see.

"How are you getting along?" He turned back to look at her. The box of apples felt cumbersome and he wanted to put them inside.

"I'm fine." She was positive Adam would come to badger her about the cow. Her peaceful evening with the McGuffey vanished. She steadied herself for the argument that was going to come.

"I see you've got a barn now."

She nodded. "Would you mind very much," his eyes pleaded, "if I come in and put the box on your table? They're getting a little heavy," he asked kindly and jiggled the box.

"Oh." She felt foolish. She hadn't received a visitor before now. She had a flash remembering how she had received guests at the Johnsons'. "I'm so sorry. I'm being rude. Please, come in."

"Not at all," he encouraged. She'd let him inside! He was happy, but then he saw she was twisting her hands together. She was worried, no doubt, that her brother would show up. He'd say what he had to say quickly, and leave.

"I was wondering, Lizzie," he had that pleading look again, "if you would like to go to the dance this Saturday."

She shook her head so fast he nearly missed it. "I won't be able to go." She hoped she said it gently. He seemed such a pleasant man and she liked him. It was hard to tell him no. *Once in a lifetime is enough.*

"Do you ever get away from here?" he implored. "Do you ever have fun?"

She thought of the cows and pigs, and the garden. She could say she liked her McGuffey Reader and being on her own in the shack.

"What if I just come by and pick you up on Saturday?"

"I won't be able to go." She prayed he would not insist, or worse, push for a reason.

"He doesn't own you, Lizzie."

She nodded. The candle suddenly flared, briefly throwing light around the room.

"Okay. I won't insist. Maybe someday we will get to dance, and I bet Hank Perkins will drop his jaw."

She took a deep breath.

"I have to know one thing, though, Lizzie. Then I'll get out of your hair."

She looked uncertain.

"Is it because you don't like me?" He squeezed his eyebrows together.

"Oh no!" she exclaimed, then jumped at her own voice and giggled. "I think I do like you!"

"Good, then." The furrows in his brow relaxed and he grinned. "You can expect to see me soon." She smiled at the wave he made with his back toward her.

"And," he exclaimed over his shoulder, "Don't worry about your brother, Lizzie. I'll handle him."

"I'll do that myself," she answered back.

The snows started early that year. On October 31, midday, the clouds darkened, and a warning north wind howled. Tiny pellets, hard and dry, spat from a sullen sky. Adam told Lizzie, who was making bread, to get back to her shack and take care of the animals. She directed Johanna's motionless daughters to get the bread out of the oven before it burned.

For three days the snow toyed with them. It was brittle and angry the first day, making tempers snap. Lizzie wore a path between the two places, trying to stay even with the chores. The second day, the sun came out to tease them before heavy flakes started plopping, fragments from an exploding sky.

Lizzie's path between the shacks got obliterated within moments.

On the third day there was a sugary confection at Lizzie's door. She was behind schedule because the obstinate stove refused to stay lit. She put on her boots and coat in haste and didn't attend to laces or buttons. She was not surprised Adam was already at the barn waiting for her.

He barked at her. "When you're done, come and help me dig out the hay under the snow pile." By the time he and the horse were out of the yard, snow sprites enveloped them and swallowed them whole.

She did not observe the visitor who went into her shack after Adam rode off. She was irritable with the animals in the barn, fretful about her stove, and imagining a miserable cold night ahead of her. One milk cow champed, responding to her gruffness with bellows. "Come on," she snapped at its big-eyed indifference and tucked her icy hands under her armpits.

She smelled the smoke drifting from her fire as she headed toward the shack. *Well, at least that's a relief.* She could warm her fingers before they got freezing cold again digging out the hay.

The wind caught the door and flung it open, and there inside John Herbert was coaxing the stove with the poker. "Oh," she jumped back. Behind her, a wall of white swirled like a swarm of feathery mosquitos pushing against the door, and it took the two of them to get it shut.

He brushed the snow from her coat. "When did you come?" she said quietly. He had considered she might be inclined to throw him out. "You know you really shouldn't be here."

"You've told me that before," he reminded her.

She got defensive. "I know. Adam's waiting for me to help dig out the hay."

"Why don't I go help him instead? Or, we could wait for him here. He'll come back, won't he?"

"He'll be furious!"

"Well, I don't want him to take it out on you. And I don't want to be another man telling you what to do. Far as I can see, you've had a belly full of that. So I'll do what you want me to do, Lizzie. I'll leave if you want me to. Or I'll stay, and we can face him together. Just tell me what you want, Lizzie."

"I don't know." She watched the flames of the fire licking the walls of the stove.

"Okay. Someday I think you will know, though. I hope I'm around when you do." John Herbert's words crowded in with her own since Johanna's death. She had repaid Adam in full, if payment was required. Long ago. Johanna deteriorated, and Lizzie witnessed her life drip away, oozing a droplet at a time. As life drained from the one, it seemed to flow back toward the other. She was becoming clearer. Maybe it would make sense, like John said, sooner or later.

"You afraid to face him?"

"No. I'm not afraid *of* him, John. I'm afraid *for* him. And when the time comes, I will face him—alone."

"Why would you do that? You know I will stand right with

you. If you let me."

"It's all right, John Herbert."

"But can you do it? Will you?" He wanted to add, "and when?" Instead he smiled.

"Oh yes, I will." She was touched that he cared.

"What will he do if you stand up to him?"

She shrugged. "I don't know. I'll find out soon enough. Here, put your coat on." It had been warming on the chair near the fire.

"Are you sure, Lizzie?" She stood tall, as she had at the Johnsons, not hunched over to protect herself.

The wall of snow that had followed her into the shack must have been a mirage. When she opened the door, a thin veil of sunshine stood in its place.

"It's going to be a beautiful day, John." She looked up at the clean blue sky.

He put on his hat, pulled his plaid wool scarf around his neck, and returned her smile. He had just disappeared over the ridge when she pulled off the dark head scarf and felt the warm rays heat the hair that tumbled over her shoulders.

Mrs. Andersson

She Gets Her Wish

When she applied for her patent in 1912…she had a log house, stable, chicken house, garden, and 25 acres of wheat, oats, and barley. Her homestead cabin was lovely, with two main rooms, an addition for a kitchen, and a wraparound porch. She raised Leghorn chickens but was best known for her homemade brew, reputed to be the best in the country.

Sarah Carter, editor, *Montana Women Homesteaders*

"We'll have the men put the casket against the far wall."

Bertha Wilcox and Sophie are spreading out checkered tablecloths on a long table at the opposite end of the schoolhouse room. Sophie accommodates Bertha's girth by sucking her breath in when they must make room for each other to pass between the wall and table. Their experienced hands smooth out the creases, and a few times, in their haste, Bertha's brawny shoulders accidentally knock against Sophie. Either an enthusiastic Lizzie or the organized Nora was there ahead of them. Whichever one it was must have gotten up before dawn to leave a touching bouquet of late-summer flowers. The women place the black-eyed Susans and the coneflowers in the center of the table. Two voluptuous sunflowers droop over the lip of the metal coffeepot that serves as the vase. At the table end nearest the door, a stack of plates and utensils greedily gobbles up precious space. The women wonder if there will be enough room for all the casseroles, baked goods, and desserts. Mirna Clawson will be hauling in a pot of coffee in the rig she uses to deliver her tapestries and blankets. She told Mr. Clawson to tell the ladies there will be enough for two cups of coffee for everyone, because she is going to make it in her dyeing tub.

"Mr. Clawson is bringing more chairs before he comes with the casket," Sophie reassures Bertha, who is fussing about where they are going to put everyone. She is sniffling and absently stops to wipe her nose on her sleeve. She has a handkerchief tucked up in the cuff but doesn't pull it out. In spite of the tragedy, Sophie maintains her usual optimism. "And Felix has the ones from his office." She grins at the picture of him bustling down Lewistown's main street with wooden chair legs askew and stabbing at the air.

Mr. Clawson has been devising the casket ever since the accident. Mirna hears him from her workroom over the whir of her loom. He is in the barn, mumbling and moaning, even with the nails hanging from his lips. She does not mention to him her fear about swallowing one. Although he hasn't been to bed for three nights, she gives him a hearty breakfast when he comes in for coffee. He tells Mirna he has to get it just right with the scrolls and engraving.

Mirna doesn't remind him of what Mrs. Andersson surely would say if she were present. She would no doubt tell him, "Henry, I don't want you to make no such fess over me. Keep it simple, jus' like me," and then she would give him a sweet smile with those perfectly white teeth of hers. How could she have such healthy-looking teeth when she was older than all of them?

He has been telling her privately, while he labors over his task, the reason he must do it the way he is. "Listen now, Millie, I know you wanna argue with me 'bout this, but I ain't hearin' none of it, and don't you get it up in that frosty head of yours that you're gonna come 'round and haunt me all the rest of my livelong days over it. Ya hear? There ain't no one in this here part of the world who done more for people than you. I couldn't hold up my gol-dang head, Millie, if I didn't do the best I could by you. Don't ya get it?" If she were really out there in the stall where he is banging away, he wouldn't get away with what he is doing. He knows she would command him, "Now, Henry, you listen. Make sure it is just a plain pine box. Ya hear me, Henry?" Knowing her, she'd probably want him to use the leftover ash planks from her kitchen floor.

More than one person today is going to stand up in that schoolhouse and give an account of some time or other when Mrs. Andersson had a hand in fixing something that could have turned out real bad otherwise. Just look at that Sophie and Bertha. Who would ever think those two could be in the same room together without going at each other, after Bertha and her minions attacked Sophie without just cause a few years earlier. Although it took Sophie several months to recover, the resentment is behind them. Mr. Clawson watched them earlier this morning when he went in to drop off the sawhorses where they will hold the coffin during the service. Their heads were nearly touching as they worked. They were quiet, talking in hushed voices now and again when one or the other needed help. "Millie would be pleased as hell to see that," he comforts himself.

No one knows for sure if Preacher Holmquist will perform the service. Well, of course, he does have his reasons for his reservations, him riding around the country and trying to get people on the right path, away from sin and damnation. He never could budge Mrs. Andersson from her point of view, and she couldn't bring him over to her side, even with the many slices of pie and the coffee she filled the old rover up with. Not that she fed him to try to convince him to accept what she was doing. He warned her that she would end up in calamity, and maybe the accident was proof of that point, although Brother Holmquist was referring to what was going to happen to her soul when she crossed to the other side. He wasn't much concerned about how the end came on this earthly plane. She patted his knee each time he brought it up, as though she was comforting one of those children of Adam, the German immigrant from Russia, who she doled pieces of candy out to whenever she went to visit his missus. It was the only thing she could think of to brighten their tragic-looking faces; they did not know how to cope with a mother who was permanently absent in the head. Mrs. Andersson never did shut the door on anyone, no matter how they viewed her, or how they behaved in general. Look at how she soothed the angry hearts of Bertha and Mr. Wilcox in the later years. By the time old Wilcox was put six feet under, you would have thought those two were childhood sweethearts, the way they carried on.

Truth is, no one in the county knows the half of what Mrs. Andersson had done. They only know about the later parts, once she arrived in the county in 1895 with her fresh new husband. But that was years before any of those who will be at her service today took up homesteading.

She and Henry Clawson go back the farthest. He was the one who pitched in after Mrs. Andersson's husband died, and she was left alone to run the business. He told her right at the beginning, "It don't make no bit of difference to me, Millie, what you and your husband been up to." He told her he was going to make sure she could keep on going. He wasn't a regular customer, that's for sure, because he didn't have much of a taste for liquor, although after his wife died, Millie consoled him with nips of her whiskey on some nasty winter nights when he was about as black as the inside of a coal mine. She mixed it with coffee and comfort. Stayed with him until he talked himself to sleep and drifted off in his cozy chair, the one his wife had hauled on the train all the way from Kansas when they headed for Montana. Millie wrapped warm blankets around him and put his head against a pillow so it wouldn't fall hard on his chest and jerk him awake in the middle of the night. Then, she took off back to her place where her mash was heating on the stone furnace of her still. She was very watchful to the attending of the heating and cooling of her barley mash, for she had a healthy and respectful caution about her profession. She knew the potential danger that could erupt with even the slightest neglect.

She got to be prosperous because when they opened the railroad, she started selling bottles to the Milwaukee men, and they became regular customers at her stop on their 157-mile run from Lombard to Lewistown. The "Jawbone" would pull up to her siding and toot its whistle for every gallon of homemade brew Mrs. Andersson delivered. It was good stuff, too. She had learned how to make it when she was a girl living in Georgia. She and her sister, who recently had died of old age over in Choteau County, had run off when they were fifteen and seventeen years old. But that was another story.

Mrs. Andersson was particular about her brew. She prided herself on how plump her Leghorn chickens grew, but she was assiduous about her brewing. It was a great pity she wouldn't be attending the gathering at the schoolhouse today. Her lively spirit made a fella want to jump up and do a jig, and she would be missed as much as her pot of spicy chicken thighs that she brought to every event. People lined up to get one of those meaty pieces that required a slug of water before you could come back to burn your mouth between bites. She grew the hottest little peppers around, not those squat, bland green peppers everyone else coaxed to maturity in their gardens. She knew the hot from when she lived in Georgia, and if anyone asked her, she wasn't shy about saying she wouldn't give two cents for a plain old bell pepper. "They jus' gum up the works of good ol' southern cookin'." It took her a few years to figure out how to grow hot peppers in the uncooperative climate. She discovered that the soil on the south side of the ridge running east to west on her property heated up the earliest in the spring and had Mr. Clawson build her some wooden frames there. She babied those seedlings like they were her children, tucking them up with her good cotton bedsheets on evenings when the frost threatened.

Hank Perkins, who once attempted to court Nora then got blown off course, promised he was going to play "Old Black Joe," but by god, he said, that was the only sorrowful tune he'd do. If they wanted him to play more than that, he said he wanted to do "Turkey in the Straw" or "Little Brown Jug." "Otherwise," he fretted, "Mrs. Andersson will jump down right from on high and kill me for making everybody miserable and melancholy." No one wanted him to play the last song. It just didn't seem to be in good taste, especially if Preacher Holmquist decided to attend. They asked Nora if she would talk some sense into him, her being a musician and schoolteacher. Nora wasn't sure why that was necessary, as she figured Mrs. Andersson just would be thrilled that everybody had come together for the occasion. And wouldn't she be the first to say she wanted it to be jolly and entertaining? Nora was pretty sure Mrs. Andersson would enjoy the irony of the song, too, among other things, because she was making her living all these years from her hooch. It even seemed a fitting choice, given the circumstances. Besides, Nora hadn't talked to Hank Perkins for a few years. He had decided to return to Lewistown only several months after she and Mr. Hawthorne had tied the knot. She would talk to him just to put everyone who might be offended at ease, but it seemed an empty effort, she confided to her husband, Sam. Everyone but her thought she was the right choice to talk him out of it, because if she couldn't convince him by speaking of propriety, she would eventually talk him to death, and he would concede from the fatigue.

Hank was a regular customer for Millie. But there was more to it than that. He always brought his fiddle along when he turned up around two in the morning and Millie was working the still. He couldn't sleep at home because the rheumatism in his knees hurt so damn bad he couldn't find one comfortable spot in the bed. He'd turn on his left side to ease the pain in the right knee until the left knee started "spittin' fire," he told Millie. Then it was downright hopeless to try to get any decent rest. He told her the dear Lord must be making him pay for his sins in those younger years, when he'd gotten thrown off more horses than he could count. Her brew numbed his distress, and the more he drank, the better he played. After her husband passed on, she got used to the solitude during her night's work, but Hank brought her another kind of solace when the work became tedious. When there was a full moon, particularly, the two of them would get to whistling and singing like two basset hounds, and Henry and Mirna Clawson could hear them clear over at their place.

Once she made her mash and heated it on the stone furnace, she forced the evaporated alcohol through the cap arm. It was during this process she added her secret ingredient to the thump keg. She kept her back to Hank while she was doing it if he was sitting in his usual spot, but by that time he was usually too liquored up to notice that was where her magic occurred, and what differentiated her whiskey from other distillers. For Hank, the brief reprieve from pain was about as much as anyone could hope for, and he wasn't curious about how Mrs. Andersson arrived at her potions. Most brewers wanted to get the whiskey to market quickly. Mrs. Andersson didn't like the idea of her clients getting inebriated on cheap liquor so she made three passes through the still to remove all the impurities. She wanted her customers to have as much pleasure in the drinking as she had in the brewing. She believed that quality alcohol, made with attention to detail, and with care and good sanitation, would prevent the drinker from turning nasty or mean. In Hank's case, if it eased a troubled body, that was its own reward.

On one occasion that she later chuckled to herself about and said, "Millie, Millie, you ol' fool, you," a time when old man Holmquist called on her, she took a side road off her usual manner of letting people act like they need to and in her sweet way confronted him. While he sat on her broad porch, shielded from the intense afternoon sun, devouring her cherry pie and washing it down with thick black coffee, he hammered at her again about her still and the evil it raised. She wasn't so much irked as she was tired of his insistence that he was both the holder of the only truth and its great spokesman. She wasn't even defensive, didn't raise her voice at all. She just wanted him to see another side of things, so she gently explained that when alcohol affected people's characters and transformed personalities, the reason for it was that it had been poorly produced. She tried to enlighten him by explaining that to reduce the impurities, she sent her alcohol through the process two more times than anybody else.

By the time he got on his mule and sauntered off, she was already laughing at herself. If she allowed it, she could be filled with disgust about her past life. She had just cause to hate herself and feel shame for the rest of her days. Regrets, if she let them, would tie her up so tight she would not be able to get out of bed in the morning. So, in her wisdom, even as she laid out her point of view to Holmquist, she knew it was pointless, and she wasn't going to dwell on having made the fruitless attempt. There was to be no listening on his part. His mind didn't have a room in it for compromise, for it feared the walls in the other rooms of his brain would tumble down in a heap. Imbibing of liquor was bad, he kept repeating, like a Bible verse he couldn't get off his tongue, where it was stuck. He had traveled far and wide in the course of his work, he reminded her, and had seen the effects of careless drinking on many families in the area. Mrs. Andersson said she couldn't argue that fact with him. She was right sorry that something that could be so highly enjoyable might be badly abused, and the two of them sat side by side for some time, regretting there was no common solution between them. That didn't stop him from dropping by her place and eating some more of her pie when he was traveling in the Lewistown area.

She grew her own barley. She also had twenty-five acres of wheat and oats. Henry Clawson and Arnold Steadman built a second story on her house and added a kitchen when her business started to thrive. She even had them put up a picket fence around the place, and a wraparound porch. She planted a row of cypress alongside her still to keep out prying eyes.

Mrs. Andersson asked Mirna to make a tapestry for the wall in her main room opposite the stone fireplace that spanned floor to ceiling. The men had installed tongue-and-groove strip maple flooring in there that Mrs. Andersson had ordered special from Chicago. She told Mirna to make whatever she thought would fit, trusted that she would come up with the exact colors and theme for the house and her personality. Mirna started the project with a gigantic Turk's cap lily in the right center of the tapestry, and to complement that brilliant orange, she wove double-headed red poppies, adding blue violets to the background and ground cover. Because Mirna liked to sneak surprises into her work, Mrs. Andersson laughed and clapped her hands when the finished piece was hung on the great wall and she discovered a magpie hidden in the lower left corner. He was stealing a stalk of her barley. Mrs. Andersson understood exactly why Mirna put the bird in the weaving. Several times Millie had asked Henry Clawson if he had a notion about how to keep the dang things out of her grain, for fear they would eat up all her profits before she even had a chance to get them ground into mash.

Mr. Clawson got a rare look on his face, the kind when you knew he was going to poke at you a little because you caught that twinkle there in his eyes, and his nose made a little twitch when she asked him if he had a solution. He said, "Millie, all I can tell ya is those dang magpies is social fellas. Invite 'em over on that big ol' porch of yours of an evening, break out some of that brew of yours, and see if that don't do the trick." She flashed her piano row of white teeth straight at him and said his advice was about as useful as Holmquist's demand she give up sinning and follow the straight and narrow.

She handed Mirna one hundred dollars after they hung the tapestry. Bertha Wilcox walked in during the hanging, and she and Mrs. Andersson stood in front of it oohing and aahing. They chatted like they were the busy magpies themselves as they explored the variety of flowers woven into the quiet pockets of space. Mrs. Andersson said, "My, my, Bertha, that Turk's cap lily is the same one that growed right in front of the country store down there in Georgia. It was that very same color. How did you know that, Mirna?" She turned to ask her, but Mirna had disappeared. She'd slipped into Mrs. Andersson's new kitchen to tuck the hundred dollars into her ceramic flour canister.

Bertha is sobbing so hard her shoulders are in a spasm. "Oh Bertha," Sophie puts her arms over the quaking. They have the table laid and ready, and Mr. Clawson is standing outside by the rig with Arnold Steadman. Mrs. Andersson wasn't a large lady to begin with, and there wasn't much left of her since the accident, so the coffin should be fairly easy to lift. Except that Mr. Clawson has put so much wood on the thing—adding all the decorative bits and pieces made from the leftover maple from the floors in Mrs. Andersson's main rooms—that it will take four men to get it inside the door. Thank goodness, Mr. Clawson measured the width of the schoolhouse door before he assembled the casket. He had the practical good sense to put the box on the back of his wagon before he began adding the scrollwork. He fashioned the face of a serene angel with lofty wings on the lid because, as he told Mirna, "Devil knows she had more Christian in her than most of us."

"She were my best friend," Bertha wails. Sophie pats her tenderly. "She were the one who got me and Fred back together. It were like she had one a them crystal balls. It woulda been mighty hard for me if we been enemies before he got so sick there toward the end."

"I know," Sophie nods. It was while she was convalescing at Mirna's after Bertha had knocked her off the Appaloosa, smacking her in the head with a rock, that Mrs. Andersson planted Sophie's own seed of forgiveness. She sowed it without a fuss, burying it deep inside Sophie through her cakes and soothing, and most of all, through listening. Maybe Mrs. Andersson should have been the homestead reporter writing columns back to Chicago, instead of Sophie. But she didn't ever learn to read or write. She could sure listen, though. She must have had just about everybody's story carried around in that heart of hers, and yet, like Bertha, each one was convinced that they were Mrs. Andersson's best friend.

Most everyone had advised Sophie while she convalesced to snatch up that young Felix while he was of a mind, before he turned tail and headed back to Chicago. She had healed enough to take frequent visits to town in the buggy with Mr. Clawson. He would put her down at Mr. Hendrickson's and head on to the livery, and by the time he came back to retrieve her, five or six people had laid out to her the practical, not to mention financial, reasons to be married. "He's such a sensible fellow," they pointed out to her.

But not Mrs. Andersson, who came to sit with her every single day for the three weeks she was laid up. If Sophie was awake and started to moan, Mrs. Andersson put that dark arm of hers over Sophie's sweet white hand, and she patted it. Sometimes she'd hum, "Shoo, Fly, Don't Bother Me," to which Sophie would open her eyes and grin. During the last week of her convalescence, Sophie was sitting up in bed drinking tea, and her doubts and worries about marrying Felix started to spill out. She had not spoken her thoughts aloud before, nor had she mentioned them to herself. "It just means so much to me, Mrs. Andersson, to write about the stories of the people here." She was afraid marriage would tie her to a family and a husband who expected her to live a conventional life. "I want to be as free as you are."

It wasn't so much about Felix that she had questions, she explained. Still she was worried, even after the hullabaloo with Bertha, about losing her independence. She needed to be her own person, she told Mrs. Andersson, "Just like you are." She nodded. "You make your own way, don't you, and you do so well." She said she had the strongest yearning to live out her lifelong days in this harsh world, and she would be satisfied writing a weekly column and learning how to handle a farm. She liked the solitude; she even liked the four corners of her shack.

Mrs. Andersson did not reveal to her during this intimate moment the ins and outs of her own early single life. She never did tell a soul about that, although she almost mentioned it to Bertha when Bertha was in such a state over Fred because he went after other women. Although she could have acted like Sophie's other advisers, pointing out the difficulties for single women, she whispered to her that she was a smart girl with a good head, and she would make the right choice when the time came.

"You doing okay, Mrs. Wilcox?" Felix stammers, nearly lurching through the doorway with his chairs. Sophie squeezes Bertha's shoulders once again then assists her favorite lawyer with his awkward burden. With his three, that made thirty chairs, including the ones Mr. Clawson brought.

"Sophie, did you really need my chairs?" Felix interrogates her as he looks about the crowded room. She throws him a stern glance then shrugs when she sees there is only room for two more of them inside. They've reserved one open spot between the casket and the table for Mr. Holmquist to stand, if he shows up.

As much as Felix sometimes irks her when he makes a thoughtless comment, Sophie feels sympathy for him after a moment. He's parked himself on his chair, outside the door like the teacher has put the dunce in the corner, and she comes out after him. She hates mothering him, which she realizes is sometimes required, but thinks it is necessary at this moment, for Felix cannot reconcile his feelings about what has happened to Mrs. Andersson.

The problem for Felix is that one day, less than one month ago, Mrs. Andersson marched into his office and declared she wanted to make out a will. "At once!" she had demanded. And he nearly jumped up out of his lawyer chair and saluted her, she was that adamant. She said she had decided after watching him these past few years that he was a good soul, just the kind of boy she would have liked to have for a son, if she'd ever had one. She told him that she was getting up in years then laughed and said, "Not supposin' you noticed," and that if and when the time came for her to wrap it up here and head on to that other world, at which juncture she pointed downward, she wanted things tidied up in a neat bundle. "No need for no loose ends to confuddle everyone."

The two of them sat in his office for half the day. She'd brought a bit of the latest brew—which had a hint of blackberry in it—for him to try, and between them sampling the whiskey and gathering together her assets, it was past suppertime before they wrapped things up. People walking by the office heard infectious giggling, first from her, then him, as if they were having a party. What they didn't hear were the tears dropping between the laughter that afternoon.

Just being around Mrs. Andersson, whiskey or not, could be so lively you could almost forget that you had any woes. One homesteader, several years before, who had taken up land a few miles from her place stopped by in his sorrows to say good-bye. He said he was giving up because he had run out of money. Anyone witnessing that occasion would not believe that when he left her that day he was smiling like he had discovered gold nuggets up in the Little Belts. He even promised to write to her when he got back to Minnesota. "Don't read," she hollered after him. "Don't matter none," he yelled in return.

He did write to her often and as recently as a month ago, and each time she received a letter she hurried over to Mr. Clawson to have him read it to her. The homesteader had done quite well since moving back to Minneapolis, where he opened an apparel shop. He even sent Mrs. Andersson an aqua-colored shawl to "keep you warm on them chilly nights," he said, "when you're out tending to your business." She put it around her shoulders only on the occasions when there was a chill in the air and she entertained guests out on her porch.

Since the accident Felix has eaten very little and is visibly shaken. Because he wrote up the will for her, he is convinced that he must be responsible for the fact that she unexpectedly died. Almost everyone has been trying to console him, and if

Mrs. Andersson were alive, she would surely talk him out of that nonsense. She would say, "Now, now, Felix, you and me both know that is a bunch of donkey poop," or some other thing like that, and before you know it, Felix would be chuckling. Sophie is going to have to do some hard work to get even a slim smile from him for a while.

Well, it is likely he is feeling this way because during the middle of writing up her will, Mrs. Andersson confided her colorful story to Felix. It wasn't because he was a lawyer and sworn to secrecy. At least that's what she said when they were sipping and yakking and discovering how much they liked each other. It started to slip out at the point when she said she hoped her son was at least a little like him. At first he thought it was the whiskey talking, for earlier she had said *if* she had a son, but being a lawyer he needed to go back to check the facts. He said, "Mrs. Andersson, I need to clarify if you actually do have a son now, for that may weigh on how we proceed." Well, doggone it, that's when the tears started.

And wouldn't you know it, at that very moment Nora came rushing into the office as if Felix only had his business open on rare occasions. She saw the two of them sitting there, half pie-eyed, not realizing Mrs. Andersson was right in the middle of a sorrowful tale, and said she'd come back later. Well, Felix sort of jumped up from his leather chair, but he wasn't quite stable, and it started to roll out behind him. He lurched forward and nearly fell flat on his face on his desk. This was too much for Nora. She didn't know whether she should be laughing or running out the door, but then Mrs. Andersson started to giggle, and then she couldn't stop laughing. Between outbursts, she waved Nora over. "Sit down, sit down, Nora. Have a drink." Nora accepted. "Just the one," she said, for she was thinking about the vegetables in the stew she had on the stove. If there is one thing she cannot abide, it is mushy carrots and potatoes.

After Mrs. Andersson managed to get the giggles under control, Nora told Felix, "I just came to talk to you about Jessie Mae." But Nora was not one to make a single statement. She believed in extended explanations to make sure no thought wandered into neglect.

Felix was amazed. For the life of him he couldn't figure what in the wide world possessed two women at the same moment to come to his office to take care of legal business. Mrs. Andersson had recovered her normal cheerful self and asked how Jessie Mae was getting on at the schoolhouse. Nora is so proud of that granddaughter of hers, she forgot she was only going to take one drink and was quite enjoying the flavor of that blackberry in her whiskey, so it wasn't until Sam arrived looking for her that she remembered her meaty pot going soggy at home. She told Felix she would return "to take care of some serious business," and gave a prolonged wave, grinning at the two of them while Sam supported her out the door, holding her other elbow.

Nora and Sam Hawthorne were two of Mrs. Andersson's faithful customers. They are not excessive imbibers, but they enjoy a good glass in the evening while Sam reads to Nora. They are cozy in their matching rockers in front of their fireplace. One of Mirna's thick rugs keeps their feet warm even when a chilling Charles Dickens tale or an Arctic blast releases gloom and bleakness into the room. On warm summer evenings they often called on Mrs. Andersson, and the three of them sat on the wraparound porch while Mr. Hawthorne read about a poor kid in the workhouse who was deprived of even his gruel. They didn't notice when Mrs. Andersson's eyes turned wet, for when that happened, she generally went into the kitchen to retrieve hard cheese and bread.

When Nora arrives at the schoolhouse and spies Felix sitting outside on a chair, she limps up to him and suggests that he conduct the service for Mrs. Andersson in case Mr. Holmquist does not appear. Even before the accident, Sophie recognized from how Felix behaved following his meeting with Mrs. Andersson that something very private occurred in his office. Felix is too principled to reveal even to her a dead person's story told behind closed doors. When he starts sobbing, the two women glance at each other. Sophie pats his shoulder, and Nora shrugs hers. Besides Felix, only Nora and Jessie Mae are comfortable standing in front of people and making speeches. Nora shrugs again and whispers to Sophie, "I will do it if the preacher doesn't come," and pats her on the arm.

By now, everyone has heard from one source or another how the accident occurred. Mr. Steadman is the mechanical genius around Lewistown. The loom he built for Mirna is one among many marvels he has devised. His skill in designing creative inventions lies in part in his practice of taking things apart. Mr. Steadman often undoes things, and in the process of stripping them down to a last nail, he always learns something.

It took Mr. Steadman a few hours of investigative work, winding parts in reverse, to determine why the still blew up. No one questioned his assessment at pinpointing the cause except for Felix, who wrestles with what he considers the absolute truth, his truth. The real reason lies in Mrs. Andersson unburdening herself to him. He is fixed on the notion that the accident occurred because either she didn't care to go on living anymore, or else she could not contain her feelings after her confession. The end result was that she didn't apply her rigorous caution as the vapors passed through the worm into the worm box. That was where Mr. Steadman said the trouble had started and ended. It was senseless to apply a motive to what happened, the neighbors told Felix. "Certainly," they consoled him, "it was not your fault." Mr. Steadman said what happened was that Mrs. Andersson neglected to check the creek above the still to see if anything was blocking the flow of necessary cool water in and out of the worm box. "Some twigs," Mr. Steadman surmised, "got stuck in the thick mud about thirty yards above her place several weeks ago, it looks like. When it got to raining hard, the creek got swollen with leaves and branches and bugs. Even some rocks. What it looks like is that the water didn't slow down that much for a time, and it continued to flow through the worm box. I'd guess she didn't see the trouble coming."

There was still a question unanswered, though. It was not at all like her to distill without checking out every aspect from beginning to end. She monitored the changes in weather conditions with great regularity, clearly aware that if the alcohol was not being cooled constantly by the creek water and circulating around the coil, the gas would build up too much pressure. That is what happened to her mother down in Georgia and left her and her sister teenage orphans.

It is a fact that Montanans consider the weather front-page news every day, chiding it for being either too hot, too cold, too dry, too wet, dark too early, or for having too much snow, too little moisture, too many gray days, too much sun, too few dark hours. The wind is incessant, so there is no need to mention it independent of other conditions. When the weather is brought up, it is the second part of an exchange between neighbors after the preliminary greetings. Not so with Mrs. Andersson. "What's the weather lookin' like for tomorrow, Henry?" she'd ask, riding onto the Clawson farm. "And good afternoon to you, Millie," Mr. Clawson would tip his hat at her and call back, laughing. "Oh, you." She'd grin and then wait until he offered his seasoned weather opinion. She became a good assessor of weather conditions over the years but looked to Henry Clawson for a second valuable opinion.

No, she was not one to take unnecessary chances, to not scout out and maintain her water source. Someone suggested that perhaps it was because her years had been catching up with her. The stream was lined with thick bushes in some places, and it was getting harder to lift those aging legs through thickets and high grasses. Maybe she just didn't see the dam building up because her eyesight was failing, which was, of course, possible. Nora was the first to think of that, since her own vision had begun deteriorating following her spill off her horse into the crevasse, which broke her leg and left it shorter when it healed. If it weren't for Sam, she would miss out on her favorite classics and his Charles Dickens.

Felix replied, "It wasn't her eyesight." He wanted to add that she was spryer than some of the ladies who were many years her junior, but Sophie shook her head as though she knew what might tumble out and offend.

"Now listen, young Felix," Mr. Clawson says to him as people begin arriving early for the service and searching to find a special spot to place their casseroles and biscuits. There is pride in the humble offerings contained within those dishes. They represent the feelings toward Mrs. Andersson that cannot be spoken. "I wanna talk to you for a minute, here." Mr. Clawson takes Felix by the sleeve, leads him outside, and sits him down on the wooden swing at the corner of the schoolyard.

"It's no good, Mr. Clawson," Felix tells him. "I already know you are going to tell me, like all the rest, that it isn't my fault about the accident." He's staring toward the mountains that rise up from out of the flat land, looking like prehistoric beasts hiding under brown dirt, peeking out between sparsely spaced trees.

"Well, doggone it, young man, that ain't what I am gonna tell ya! This here life is chock full of surprises. You and me know that, don't we, young fella?" Felix gives him a wide stare that makes his blue eyes appear like giant balls through the thick lenses, but he says nothing.

"Now take a look at you and Sophie. Just for example, I mean."

"What about us?"

"Well, I ain't meanin' to say there's somethin' wrong. No,

that's not what I mean at all. But goodness knows you two was the unlikeliest pair anybody ever saw comin' out here to homestead. Ever'body shook their heads on that one. Remember when you couldn't get up on that gol-dang Appaloosa when you first got here? Well, dang it. People was 'bout ready to line up and make bets on how long you'd last." Except for Mirna who, had she spoken aloud, would have told the doubters she was 100 percent positive they would thrive. Survival means making adjustments to what life throws in your way.

"They were?" Felix squints at Mr. Clawson. *Of course they were going to make it. Why would anyone have thought different?*

"Now, listen, I ain't meanin' to tell you what to think or feel about Mrs. Andersson's calamity. I know you got plenty of other people puttin' in their wooden nickel."

"Yes sir, Mr. Clawson, I sure do. Miss Nora just asked me to be the substitute if Preacher Holmquist doesn't come."

"And you think you ain't up to doin' it? Is that it?"

"I know I'm not."

"Now, you may think different when I'm done tellin' you somethin'. That's why I got you away from the others, so's I could lay things out for you truthful wise. And what I'm 'bout to tell you is somethin' that I learnt about Millie a few years back, and Mirna is the only other one to know 'bout it. Except I figure that's what Millie told you, ain't it?" He squints at the usually self-assured lawyer.

"I don't know." Felix's brow wrinkles, trying to imagine that he and the Clawsons share the same secret about Mrs. Andersson, for she said she hadn't ever told another soul and didn't know why she was doing so that day. She giggled afterward and awkwardly put her hand on the young man's shoulder. "It musta been the blackberry I mixed in with the brew."

"Wasn't it about that there business down there in Denver?"

"You know about that?" Felix's eyebrows rise over the rims of his glasses.

"Well, heck yeah, Felix. We've knowed about it for more'n five years."

"But she said she hadn't told another soul."

"No doubt she was tellin' you the truth, too. Way she saw it, she never did talk to no one 'bout it. See, I found out 'bout it because this roamin' cowboy came wanderin' through and did a spot of work for me one summer. Well, Millie needed some stuff done at her house, and I took this here cowboy over there to help me. He didn't say nothin' at the time, but later on, when we was workin' together at my place, he told me 'bout Millie. Course, by then, Millie was pretty old, but he still recognized her from her younger years."

"You mean he told you about her baby and the other things going on?"

"Yeah. He weren't a gossipy fella like some of them that come through and want to spread on bad feelings thick as butter on a slab a bread. He was a quiet ol' fella. Kept to himself mostly, but I kinda got the idea he really liked Millie at one time and was glad to see she'd put her past behind her. He didn't want to rock no boat, that's for sure. I think it was the surprise of seein' her again that got him talkin'. Course, you coulda blowed me over with a feather, what he told me. But after I got ta thinkin' 'bout it, I could see how it all fit together. When I told Mirna 'bout it, she told me that what's past is past, that ever'body's got one, and to leave it sittin' right there. Mirna's always right 'bout things like that."

"Didn't Mrs. Andersson recognize the cowboy, too?"

"Far as I can reckon, Millie knowed a lot of fellas 'bout that time. The ol' cowboy told me it was her and her sister who was down there in Denver. They ended up there after they'd run away from Georgia. Lord knows how they ended up there, but they probably heard about free land like all the rest of us done."

"I wonder whatever happened to the son. Did the cowboy know?"

"Well, you know the part about Mr. Andersson kidnapping her first, don't ya?"

"Yes. She said he swooped her out of that dance hall one night when it was just closing. Another man kidnapped her sister that same night. She said they were still in their dance costumes when Mr. Andersson jumped out of nowhere and threw his long-tailed canvas duster over her to cover her up. Apparently, the other sister ended up over in Choteau County."

"Yep. I reckon the two men split up after they got into Montana. Andersson musta rode Millie right up here to his cabin, and by golly, I don't think they ever made it official. I mean with a wedding and all."

"Well, in legal terms they probably weren't allowed to."

"That so? Probably is the case, ain't it?"

Hank Perkins has started fiddling "Old Black Joe" inside the schoolhouse. "But did the cowboy know whatever happened to her son?"

"All's he knowed was that one day Millie disappeared. He didn't know till later she'd been kidnapped. Never knew where she ended up till he showed up here and saw her. But three weeks 'afore she left, her little boy disappeared. They never found him. But she musta told you that."

Nora's voice rises above the others, and for a moment she sounds like a young Lillian Russell.

> *Gone are the days when my heart was young and gay,*
> *Gone are my friends from the cotton fields away,*
> *Gone from the earth to a better land I know,*
> *I hear their gentle voices calling, "Old Black Joe."*
>
> *Chorus*
> *I'm coming, I'm coming, for my head is bending low.*
> *I hear those gentle voices calling, "Old Black Joe."*

The music floating out to the swing set is somber, nearly pitiful. "What the heck is that noise?" Mr. Clawson jumps up. "Come on, Felix, we gotta put a stop to this."

Preacher Holmquist has proceeded to scolding already. There

are no empty chairs, so the two men squeeze in behind the last row. Bertha is outside the open door, sitting in Felix's chair fanning herself, wiping her eyes and rocking back and forth. "What will I do now?" she repeats. "Now, now, Bertha," Mr. Clawson touches her shoulder as they walk past.

As yet, Holmquist has not had enough time to land on Mrs. Andersson's sin as local supplier of spirits to those who cannot resist the temptation of alcohol. The group twitches nervously, however, expecting him to launch into a tirade. A tapestry hangs behind the preacher. In it the many types of local wildflowers are represented, and peeking out among the flowers are Hank Perkins, Nora and Sam, Bertha and Fred, Jessie Mae, Felix and Sophie, Mr. Clawson, Mr. Steadman, Mr. Hendrickson from the general store. There are others, Lizzie and John Herbert, Adam and his children, the homesteader who lives in Minneapolis now, Preacher Holmquist with his Bible, and next to him Mirna and her faithful Dog, who holds his bone and peers from behind the face of a dazzling sunflower. Mirna aptly has picked flowers that fit with each person, and the array is as colorful and unique as the persons who make up their community. In the center, with all her friends and acquaintances surrounding her, Mrs. Andersson glows, that perfect row of shining teeth grinning as she did in life, and at this moment, it is as if she is sitting among them. *How did Mirna find the time to make the tapestry in the short time since Mrs. Andersson's unexpected passing?* people wonder.

Mr. Holmquist gets wound up. His scolding is becoming more pointed. He has called out some recent sins of two people in the community, and it is only a matter of time before he starts on Mrs. Andersson.

"Thank you, Preacher Holmquist." Felix jumps out from the back wall where he just made himself comfortable. "We are so glad you could be here to celebrate the life of our dear friend, Mrs. Andersson," and with his long strides he reaches the center of the room in less than ten steps.

There is a collective heave of relief, and people sink into the backs of their chairs.

"Hello, everyone." Felix catches his breath, then he realizes the eyes of the room are on him. In the front row, Sophie and Nora sit side by side with their elbows locked together. He is not able to produce another word. For a moment people watch him and wait expectantly; then they start to squirm. Some clear their throats, another whistles under his breath.

"Why, we was just outside talkin', weren't we?" Mr. Clawson says as he strides up to stand by Felix. "We was wonderin' what anybody could say today about our Millie that would make us feel better with her passin'. Lord knows, 'scuse me, Preacher, she would tell us to just git on with it, wouldn't she, Bertha? Come on up here, old girl."

Bertha fiercely shakes her head. "I'll just stay out here, Henry." She sobs outside the door, but Mr. Clawson goes back and pulls her up to the center. Now there are three of them up there. "Sophie, you'd better come on up here, too. And what about you others?"

Then chairs start rumbling as wooden legs rub against each other and scrape the floor, for neighbors and friends are bolting out of them to form a circle around Mr. Clawson and the rest. "I'm gonna tell you somethin' 'bout Millie that been troublin' her awhile," he announces after everyone has pushed in as close as they can. Felix's head jerks up, his face in horror. Sophie almost gasps. Mr. Clawson grins at Felix and winks, and the room hushes.

"Now you all know Millie woulda wanted us to have us a party today. Ain't that so, Mirna? Hank, she'd want you to pull out that old fiddle of yours and get us all wound up, and what I'm thinkin' is that first of all, we should get all these dang chairs moved outside. That all right with our two schoolteachers, Nora and Jessie Mae? And then we oughta tackle all them good dishes the ladies brung here today and drink my Mirna's delicious coffee. Dang it, it's too bad Millie ain't here to supply the whiskey," at which the group bursts out laughing, except for Preacher Holmquist, who hasn't figured out quite yet what happened to the sermon he was winding up to give. He's got some scores to keep, but no one wants to do the tallying.

"Now, Bertha, I know doggone well you wanna be cryin' here today. Bawlin' your eyes out. Ain't that so? Well, dang it, we all do. I tell ya, except for my Mirna, there ain't one other person in the world I cared more for. It's a real stinkin' tragedy the way that woman had to go, blown all to pieces when she's right in the middle of makin' somethin' tasty for people to enjoy. But ya know what she'd be the most upset about here today? Do ya?"

People look at each other quizzically and shrug.

"She'd be gol-dang upset that nobody is gonna be burnin' their mouths on her hot Leghorn chickens and runnin' like heck to the well for water." Hank is mimicking him on the fiddle in the background. Some of the women already are drifting over to the table and are beginning to uncover dishes. The kids are slipping outside to play on the chairs. Nora has removed the bouquet of flowers from the table and placed them on the casket.

"So, I got a question for you 'bout Millie," Mr. Clawson continues. "You ladies over there by the food bucket listenin' to me?" They lift their heads and nod.

"Well, 'bout three years gone, Millie come to me askin' a favor. She's thinkin' 'bout the day she's gonna die, she tells me. And I say to her, 'Now, Millie, don't go and get sentimental on me, ya hear?" He winks at Felix again. "'Cuz what I think is she's gonna ask me to take her still over or somethin'.'"

The group chuckles about that. Mr. Clawson's dislike of alcohol, which he says doesn't agree with him, is common knowledge, as is his belief that drinking it will make him want to punch anybody in the mouth who's around. Mrs. Andersson tried once to explain that this was simply because it wasn't her whiskey he had tested.

"But it weren't that," he continues after the laughter dies down. "She asks me, she says, 'Henry, when my times comes, I want you to bury me by my still, if it's still around,' and I say to her, 'Well, Millie, don't you wanna be buried with all your friends in the cemetery? Do you like that precious still more than your neighbors?'"

The women at the food table look up in unison as though Mr. Clawson might say she did tell him she liked it more than them.

He says, "Well, she's got this serious look on her like somebody's already died, which concerns me, and she says to me, 'Now Henry, I don't reckon there's no other colored people buried over there, is there?' Well, heck, I tell her, I don't have no idea 'bout that. But I figured it was probably true.

"She says, 'I don't want no ruckus 'cuz some lawman says they don't allow no coloreds buried there.' So dang it, I made a deal with her that day. I says to her, 'Millie, if there's even one single person who don't want you buried in that cemetery, I will bury you by that dang still of yours, but by golly, I ain't gonna be happy 'bout it.'"

Faces with absent stares wait for him to continue.

"Now I got your attention, I'm askin' all a you. Is there anybody here objectin' to us puttin' Millie over there with her friends in the cemetery? 'Cuz if there is, I gotta get me goin' out to her place to get a hole dug."

The room is voiceless until Mr. Steadman speaks. It is the void that comes at the end of a surprise so remarkable it generates only silence. "I didn't think of Mrs. Andersson," he says in a deep voice, "as a colored." Heads around the room are nodding in agreement.

"Now that's exactly what I told Millie. I says to her, 'Dang it, Millie, I bet ever'one's clean forgot you is colored, and it don't make no difference no how.' Well, that was the way Millie was. She didn't wanna step on no toes." The women at the table are busy bustling around the table again. Bertha clangs a pot of Mirna's coffee against some tin cups. Even Felix wears a smile.

"Let's eat, ever'body," Mr. Clawson proclaims. "Then you can crank up that fiddle, Hank, and start on 'Little Brown Jug.' What you say, Preacher Holmquist?"

An African-American woman from Missouri, homesteader Bertie (Birdie) Brown of the Gilt Edge district of eastern Fergus County filed on her homestead in 1907 at the Lewistown land office. She stated that she was 'a deserted woman, have not seen my husband for ten years…and am head of …family.'

Sarah Carter, editor, *Montana Women Homesteaders*

About the Author

Mae Schick holds a Master's Degree in Linguistics. She founded SpeakFirst™, a language school in Tempe, Arizona, which was founded to teach English to corporate adults and their families working and living in the United States. During her time there, she designed curricula for the twelve languages taught, developing innovative teaching methods to motivate students learning a second language. In the late 1990's, she was a finalist for the Phoenix Athena Award because of her commitment to her employees. She wrote her first novel *Lila* with the hopes of shining a light on her cultural heritage as a descendant of Germans from Russia.

As a descendant of homesteaders herself, she is the author of the novel, *Lila*:

The wild 20's roars away in major cities, but not on an isolated Dakota prairie homestead where 19-year old Lila milks cows, fights with her sister Iris, bakes *Kuchen,* and takes care of their younger siblings. She is unaware that her prescribed life soon is going to change.

The charming but untamed Fischer rides to the farm and into her life shortly before events on the farm turn volatile and menacing. Almost simultaneously, Lila is introduced to both romance and violence.

Lila begins a journey filled with adventure, new companions, and hardships. She endures abandonment and rejection, and escapes danger. She discovers self-reliance, loses it then regains it, on the path to self-discovery.

A Life of Her Own

Made in the USA
Columbia, SC
19 June 2024

37281535R00117